Dagger of Flesh

Dagger of Flesh

Richard S. Prather

No part of this publication may be reproduced or transmitted in any form or by any means, electronic, or mechanical, including photocopy, recording, scanning or any information storage retrieval system, without explicit permission in writing from the Author.

This book is a work of fiction. Names, characters, places and incidents are products of the author's imagination or are used fictitiously. Any resemblance to actual events or locals or persons, living or dead, is entirely coincidental.

© Copyright 1956 by Richard S. Prather
First e-reads publication 1999
www.e-reads.com
ISBN 0-7592-0574-4

Other works by Richard S. Prather

also available in e-reads editions

Bodies in Bedlam
Find this Woman
Way of a Wanton
The Scrambled Yeggs
Everybody had a Gun

"Look at me, Mr. Logan . . ."

Her voice was a throbbing contralto—deep and soft like the blackness of her hair.
I didn't need the invitation. But it was very hard to keep my mind on business with my eyes wandering the way they did.
She let the robe slip down and arched herself against the couch, extending one long smooth leg.
"I like to be looked at, Mr. Logan. That's why I pose like this. I enjoy it. It makes me feel good."
"Me too." I grinned.
She raised an arm lazily. "Come closer . . . Mark. It is Mark, isn't it?"
"Yes." I moved closer.
I slid my hand under her waist and pulled her to me.
"Not yet." She took my hand in hers and held it. "Not yet," she whispered.
She leaned back and put her arms at her sides. Her eyes were closed, but she was smiling.
I sat staring at the strangely beautiful face, the curved, brazen whiteness of her body. Suddenly she opened her eyes. "All right," she said. "It's all right now, Mark."

Dagger of Flesh

1

For a long moment, she clung to me, whispering, her lips soft against my throat. They were not words of love, but obscenities, for she was not much given to words of love.

Then the last ripple of emotion shuddered through her flesh and she relaxed, moved away from me and lay quietly with her dark hair tangled against the pillow, her long body nearly as pale as the white sheet beneath it.

She lay on her back without the slightest trace of modesty or shame in her nakedness and stared at me from dark eyes. She didn't speak. We rarely had much to say. Her eyes closed, and in a few moments she was asleep.

A week ago we had met in a bar on Wilshire Boulevard here in Los Angeles. After the first intimate glances and tentative words, all of them charged with meaning as pointed and naked as an unsheathed sword, we had talked for a while. Then, almost automatically, we had come here to my apartment. That was the first time—it was afternoon then, too—and now, a week later, I still knew almost nothing about her.

Her name was Gladys, she was about thirty years old, and she was a married woman. That was nearly all of it—except that from the very beginning she had seemed not quite a stranger to me, as if I had known her or seen her before. She wouldn't talk about her home, her family, her life. It sometimes seemed that there was only one thing she wanted to talk about.

It was another late afternoon, and yellow sunlight slanted through the venetian blinds in the bedroom of my Wilshire Boulevard apartment, splashing alternate fuzzy bands of yellow and warm shadow across her full woman's body. I looked at her nakedness almost with disinterest, and with the slight distaste one sometimes feels for the object of passion when the passion has been satisfied. Perhaps it was more than that, because I didn't like her. She stirred and excited me, but I didn't really like her.

She lay quietly now, her only movement the regular breathing that stirred the lush, heavy curves of maturity, the warm yielding breasts barely moving and the gentle female roundness of her stomach rising and falling slightly with each slow breath. Gladys seemed voracious and predatory even in sleep; she made me think of those cannibal plants that capture live things and devour them.

I had showered and was almost dressed when she awakened. She stretched languorously, catlike.

"Mark," she said, "I die every time. I can't help it."

"You've told me. You'd better get dressed."

She laughed softly. "What a waste of time. Come here."

"It's late."

"Not that late."

I looped the knot in my tie and slid it up under my collar, then strapped on my gun harness and the Magnum and shrugged into my coat.

"What's the matter, Mark?"

"I told you. It's late." I looked at my watch. "It's after six. You've never stayed this late before."

"There has to be a first time."

"No, there doesn't." I walked over and sat on the edge of the bed. "Listen, Gladys, you know what's the matter. I don't like this. I don't like it at all."

She raised her left hand and slowly traced a line down between her breasts and over the white mound of her stomach. Smiling, she said, "You don't?"

"I don't like this sneaking around, hiding, not knowing who you are or where you live. I've told you before, I feel . . . I don't feel right about it."

She laughed. "We're adults. We're not in love with each other, and we both know it. But we—we like each other."

"I'm not sure, Gladys. I'm not sure I like you at all."

It didn't bother her. She laughed again, propped herself up on one elbow and looked at me. "You don't have to like me." Her eyes swept down the length of my body, then back to my face. "I don't even know for sure what I see in you," she said. "Six feet of something. Black curly hair, brown eyes, a very nice nose, even a Cary Grant dimple in that square chin. You should be handsome, Mark, but you're not. I don't even think you're good-looking." She put her hand on my knee, then grinned and said through her teeth, "I just don't know what I see in you."

I grinned back at her. "I know damned well what you see in me. Now get up, baby, and put on your pants." She got up, but slid over and sat on my lap. I shook my head. "I mean it, Gladys. It's time you got out."

"I think I'll stay."

"Let me ask you something just once more. You've got a husband, maybe nine kids for all I know. Isn't your husband in love with you? Don't you feel a little rotten sometimes?"

"Good God, Mark. Can't you forget the old goat for an hour? For a private detective, and a bachelor, you lug around some damned infantile notions. Can't you drop that silly Victorian conscience somewhere? We'll go to church on Sunday, if it'll make you feel better." She paused, a small smile on her lips, her arms going around my neck. "Now, Mark, let's not talk any more."

"Oh, for Christ's sake, Gladys." I pushed her away from me.

She was quiet for a few seconds, then she asked softly, "Tomorrow, Mark?"

"I don't know. I don't think so. Even private detectives have to work some time."

"Tomorrow night." It was a whisper. "I can get away."

"You mean you can sneak out."

She moved closer to me, lifted my hand and brushed it over her breast. "Tomorrow night, Mark?"

I hesitated, felt her move against me.

"We'll have the night, and the darkness, Mark," she said.

And finally, as she undoubtedly felt sure I would, I told her yes.

After she had gone I got the bottle of light Bacardi from the kitchen, poured a healthy splash into a tall glass and filled the glass with soda. Then I sat in the living room and thought about Gladys.

She was lovely enough, with a ripe and exciting dark beauty, but I'd have felt fewer twinges of what Gladys called a Victorian conscience if there'd been more honesty between us, less secrecy. And it was a one-sided secrecy. Gladys knew almost all there was to know about me. She knew I was Mark Logan, twenty-nine years old, a private detective, an ex-G.I. who had once worked up to sergeant but was three times a private. She knew I liked pork chops and Southern fried chicken, rum and soda, red lips and rumba music. And I didn't even know her last name. It was difficult to tell what she did or didn't like—except in one thing. The hell with it; she was an expert in that.

I tossed off the last of my drink and said the hell with it again. Tomorrow was another day and I had an appointment at my one-room office in the Farnsworth Building on Spring Street in downtown L.A. An old friend, Jay Weather, was in some kind of trouble.

I didn't know it yet, but so was I—at least it was starting.

2

Jay kept looking at his watch as if something important were going to happen any second. It was one minute till noon.

He glanced at me, blinking his bright blue eyes. The guy was frightened of something, and he was making me nervous. I'd known Jay Weather for a good many years, and I'd never seen him like this. I'd never seen his thin face so drawn and worried. He couldn't keep still; his hands fluttered in his lap and he kept shifting in the leather chair across from my desk. A man in his fifties, he looked ten years older now.

"Jay," I said, "you look as if you're ready to explode. What's eating you?"

He kept his eyes on his wristwatch. "Just a minute, Mark. Half a minute." His voice was tight.

I didn't say any more. He'd called me half an hour earlier, to make sure I remembered the appointment he'd made yesterday, and had said he'd be up at ten minutes to twelve. He'd come in looking worried and had talked about everything except whatever it was he really wanted to discuss with me—and now this.

Finally he took his eyes off his watch and looked at his left shoulder. "God damn," he said softly. "Damn, damn, damn."

"What's the matter?"

"Mark," he said. "You see it, Mark?"

He'd got me jittery enough to see almost anything he wanted me to, but I didn't know what he was talking about.

"See what?" I asked him.

He'd been holding his breath. Now he let it out between his lips in a small explosion that was almost a sob. "Don't you see it? Don't you see anything at all?"

I've seen people near hysteria before, and unless I was completely off base I was about to have a hysterical man in my office. I didn't say anything right away. I could see Jay across from me, even his reflection in the top of the desk I'd just finished polishing. I could see the rest of my office, the leather chairs, filing cabinets, divan, and it was all as it should be; I couldn't see anything that hadn't been there a minute before.

I said, "Take it easy, Jay. Relax, for Pete's sake. What am I supposed to see?"

"The parrot."

"The what?"

"Parrot, Mark. Don't you see it?" His face was twisted and he looked ready to crack. "Don't lie to me, Mark."

"Look, Jay," I said softly. "We've been friends a long time. Don't flip on me. What about this parrot?"

"There's one on my shoulder. There's a big, green parrot on my shoulder."

I suppose, under different circumstances, it would have been funny. It was the kind of thing you talk about later and laugh about as you recall it. But right then there wasn't a single thing about it that was funny. It's never laughable to look at a man you've known for years, a man you like and respect, and see him almost going to pieces.

No more than a week or two ago I'd talked to Jay at the men's clothing store he owned here in Los Angeles, and he'd been as normal and sane as I am. Something was wrong now. I knew one thing—Jay wasn't pulling my leg. He was serious.

I got a little feathery trickle down the nerves of my spine and I said cautiously, "Should I see this parrot, Jay?"

He sighed, his thin shoulders rising and falling. "I guess not. I guess not, Mark. I must be crazy."

"Don't be stupid," I said. "Tell me about it."

"All right." He lit a cigarette with a hand that shook a little, dragged deep, glanced at his left shoulder and away quickly. Then he blew out smoke and said, "I guess you think I'm crazy, even if I'm not. Maybe I am. But, Mark, a parrot is there—" He jerked his head a little to the left, his eyes averted. "And I can see it. I can see it and feel it there. You—you can't?"

I shook my head slowly. "No. But don't let it get you, Jay. I don't understand—"

He broke in, "I don't understand either. If I'm not insane I will be before long. Every damn noon, right on the dot."

"All the time?"

"No. At noon. For an hour. Never fails. Right on the dot, at noon . . ." His voice trailed off and he dragged on the cigarette.

"How long's it been going on?"

"Since Monday. Every day."

This was Thursday. That meant Jay had been going around for three days with this thing, whatever it was, digging at him. I said, "You talk to anybody else about this?"

He shook his head. "When it happened the first time—Monday—I was in the shop. Damn thing was just—just there all of a sudden. I went home. All of a sudden, at one o'clock it disappeared." He shook his head, his face lined and puzzled. "It just disappeared."

I didn't know what to say to him. We'd been friends for a long time. Not really close, but good enough friends. We hadn't seen a lot of each other lately, but I liked him and I knew he liked me.

Jay and I talked a while longer and he seemed to calm down as the minutes went by. As far as he could tell, he said, there was no reason at all for him to suddenly start having hallucinations; no shocks, no warning of any kind, no idea why it had started.

I got up and went to the big window behind my desk and looked down at Spring Street. It was crowded now with people going to lunch, cars creeping slowly up the street. Bright sunshine slanted down and glanced off the streetcar tracks. It seemed strange that everything should be going on outside as usual while we were having a conversation about an invisible parrot here in the Farnsworth Building. It was the wrong kind of day for it. The air was too bland and clear, the sun too bright outside my office window. Even the smog that usually blurs the streets of Los Angeles was high and thin. It should have been a day of whimpering winds, or fog curling around the buildings.

I turned. Jay was looking at his left shoulder. He said softly, "You know, I can see him. I can see him just as plain. He's there, I tell you. I can feel him." He cocked his head on the side. "I don't know what's real—Mark, you think I'm crazy?"

"You're not crazy, Jay. Get that out of your head." There was a chance he was, but I'd have been a fool to tell him so. He looked at me as I went back and sat down in the swivel chair behind my desk.

Then he reached into his inside coat pocket, took out a long envelope and put it on the desk. I glanced at the name stamped in the upper left corner:

"Cohen and Fisk, Attorneys at Law." Jay took some papers out of the envelope and handed them to me.

"Look at this," he said. "Here's why I came up. The other reason, anyway. I came up to see you as a friend, Mark, not just because you're a detective. Main reason is I can trust you."

"Sure, Jay. Anything I can do," I said. He seemed fairly calm now. Still nervous, but a lot better than he had been. I picked up the top paper and looked at it. For a minute I thought I was reading the thing wrong. It said: *I hereby assign, transfer, and sell all my rights, title, and interest in and to the following described property* . . .

I looked up. "What the devil is this, Jay? This is a bill of sale. It doesn't make sense."

"Yes it does. I'm selling out."

It was a bill of sale, all right, and the description was of Jay's store on Ninth Street. It must have been worth a mint.

"I don't get it," I said. "Why?"

He took a deep breath and his cheeks puffed out as he exhaled. "I've got some trouble. Some kind of trouble—unless I'm imagining it, too." His lips twisted in a wry grin. "Don't know what's real and what isn't since this— Anyway, there's a couple guys come in every night at closing time. Trying to buy the place."

"You don't want to sell, do you?"

He hesitated. "Funny thing, I do, sort of. They want me to sell for twenty-five thousand."

"Twenty-five—why, the business must be worth four or five times that, Jay."

"Closer to a quarter of a million. I carry a big stock, you know. Thing is, I . . . I want to sell to them. I can hardly keep from doing it when they come in. I'm so mixed up, it's as if I had to. I'm afraid maybe I will sell."

"You're afraid? Then what're these papers? Why—"

"I'm going to sell it to you, Mark."

"To me? Hell, Jay, I haven't got—"

"For a dollar."

I looked at him. Maybe the guy *was* crazy.

He said, "It's a favor to me, if you want to go through with it. You won't have to do anything about the business; I'll be around. This is just on paper." He paused, then went on, "These two men who've been after me—they scare me. I'm afraid they'll get rough. One of them carries a gun."

This was getting closer to the kind of thing I'm used to. Tough boys. I was starting to understand. Part of this was getting clearer.

Jay went on. "This is too much for me, Mark. I'm afraid maybe there's something wrong with me, anyway. And now this deal about the business."

He licked his lips. "And they're rough. Shoved me around a little last night. Said I'd have to make up my mind soon. Tonight, maybe."

I let that sink in. "You mean shoved you around physically? Actually roughed you up, Jay?"

"Uh-huh. They're big guys. About your size. Said if I didn't sell they'd take care of me."

I was starting to burn. Jay was all of five-seven, and fifty-eight years old. He carried around a little potbelly and was as mild as anybody I knew.

I asked him, "Want some help there?"

He nodded. "That's the deal with those papers. If things work out you can sign back the shop to me. If things don't work out for me, you can see that Ann gets the place. Look at me. Do I look as if I can handle this mess? Hell, I can hardly sell a pair of pants the way I am. There's a check in the mail for you no matter what."

"Knock that off, Jay. You don't need to pay me. And what do you mean, if things don't work out?"

"You know. Anything might happen."

"Nothing's going to happen. I think I get the deal, though. I'll be the new owner as far as the tough boys are concerned, and I'll be able to prove it. I'll have a talk with these guys, and as soon as things calm down a little you step back in. Right?"

He nodded. "If you'll do it."

"Of course I will, if you're sure you want it this way."

"I'm sure. And, besides, I really want to sell. Maybe I can relax a little then. It's been on my mind."

So far this whole conversation had seemed crazy to me, but I played along. "What do you want me to do?"

"The guys who want to buy will come back at five tonight. Want to see them—as the new owner?"

"I'll be there. What about these papers? Do we fill the things out here, so they look legal?"

He shook his head. "It may *be* legal. I checked with the lawyers yesterday and found I should run a notice of intended sale in one of the county newspapers for seven days before the sale. But a week ago I hadn't even considered it, and I didn't really decide to do this till last night. I haven't any creditors at the moment, though—all paid up. And I haven't dated the bill of sale yet; just sign it and it's done. Do it right here in the office." He smiled. "Give me a dollar, Mark; you're buying a quarter-million-dollar business for one buck."

I had to smile, myself, and he looked at me and laughed out loud. We sat there laughing at each other for a few seconds, then he turned his head and looked at the parrot I couldn't see, and he stopped laughing and said softly, "You son of a bitch."

In five more minutes the job was done and the deal wrapped up, but we sat talking. Jay asked me if I'd shot anybody lately. I told him and he swallowed strenuously.

I'd been to Jay's house only a few times, usually meeting him at a downtown bar for a drink, so I asked him about his family. He was a widower whose wife had died in childbirth. Jay's daughter, Ann, would be somewhere around twenty now. She'd never been around when I'd called at Jay's, so all I remembered of her was a scrawny kid about ten or eleven years old who always gave me a pain, and had once kicked me vigorously in the shin just for fun.

Jay had remarried a little over two years back, and I had met his new wife just once, briefly, about a year ago. I was thinking about that meeting and my mouth suddenly started getting dry. I was remembering now; only a little, but enough.

I was almost afraid to ask it, but I said, "How's . . . how's the wife, Jay?"

"Gladys? Same as usual. You met her once, didn't you, Mark?" He went on, his voice droning pleasantly, but the sound seemed to swell and fade in my ears and I didn't have any idea what he was saying.

Gladys. Even before I'd asked him, I knew. I had suddenly remembered why Gladys had seemed familiar to me from the beginning. I had remembered, vividly for that one moment, my first sight of her when she'd opened the door for me at Jay's a year ago. I'd even remembered thinking then that she was one of those wide-eyed brunettes who ripen at about eighteen and then get riper, and riper, and riper—and that Jay was going to have trouble with that one.

"What's the matter, Mark?"

"What? Oh, I'm sorry, Jay. I was . . . a million miles away." I tried to grin at him. "Say it again."

"I said it won't be long now." He glanced at his watch. "Almost one."

He kept staring at his watch while I looked at him, feeling utterly rotten. The business with Gladys had bothered me before, but it was worse now. Gladys wasn't simply a desirable woman married to some unknown male—she was Jay's wife. I thought about that for what seemed a long time.

Jay looked up suddenly and sighed. "Gone," he said. "Gone. Oh, boy." He grinned happily at me. "I'm sane for another twenty-three hours. Well, Mark, how's it feel to own Weather's?"

"No different, Jay."

"I feel better than I've felt for a week. Seems like one hell of a load off my mind. You'll be down at five?"

"Sure. I'll come down a little early. Anything you want me to do before then?"

"No. I'm all right, if that's what you mean. And thanks. Don't forget, you've got a check coming." I opened my mouth to argue, but he cut me off. "No arguments, Mark."

He got up, nodded and said, "See you about five," and walked out almost jauntily. I watched him go and wondered about him. I wondered a little about me, too. I was one fine, upstanding, hell of a bastard.

I slammed the door hard, sending echoes down the corridor, then went back to my desk, looked up the Jay Weather residence in the phone book, and dialed. A girl's voice answered, a happy, bright voice.

I told her I wanted to speak to Mrs. Weather.

"Half a minute." I heard the phone clatter, then silence—and then the voice I remembered.

"Hello, Gladys," I said. "This is Mark."

"Why, Mark! You darling. Couldn't you wait?"

"Yeah, I can wait. Gladys, forget tonight. Forget every night from now on."

"What?" She was silent for several seconds, then she said quietly, "How did you know where to call me, Mark? What's this all about? Have you been sneaking around spying on me?"

"No. I'm through, that's all. We're washed up."

"You listen to me, Mark Logan—"

I interrupted her. "Listen, Gladys, I'll say it once fast, and then that's the end of it. I know your name, and I know your husband. I like him. It wouldn't ever be the same again. I'm sorry, really, but that's how it is."

Her voice got higher, sharper. "Why, you sneaking bastard. You virtuous, Victorian, simple, stupid—"

There was more, quite a bit more, and finally I hung up. I sat and smoked for a while, thinking about Gladys, and about Jay's friendship and trust; then I forced those thoughts out of my mind and concentrated on the business at hand. I had tried to act as if nothing about Jay had been too peculiar, but now I tried to figure out whether or not the guy was really off his nut. Sane people don't go around seeing nonexistent parrots and casually selling businesses. Or do they?

I walked over to the window and looked down at Spring Street. To my right, on a projecting ledge of the building, a mangy pigeon cocked a beady eye at me and blinked. It was a lousy-looking pigeon. I wondered what I looked like to the pigeon. I wondered what that parrot had looked like to Jay.

When I found myself wondering what Jay had looked like to the parrot, I went back to my desk and put in a fast phone call to City Hall and Bruce Wilson, police psychiatrist.

3

Bruce came on, speaking in the easy, relaxed voice that matched the rest of his personality.

"This is Mark," I told him.

"Hello, Mark. How's the subconscious?"

"How the hell should I know?"

"That's the right answer, chum. What you want?"

"I need some help. Answer me this: what would make a guy suddenly start seeing things that aren't there?"

"What kind of things?"

"Well, a parrot. Why would a guy start seeing a parrot on his shoulder?"

"Don't know."

"Come on, Bruce. What might make something like that happen?"

I could almost see him squeezing his sharp chin between thumb and forefinger. "Hard to say, Mark. You serious? Or is this a hypothetical case?"

"Serious. Guy I know. Friend of mine."

"Not a lush, is he?"

"Uh-uh. Drinks, but no more than I do, as far as I know."

"Hard to say without seeing the man. Tell me more about it."

"Started Monday at noon. And it's been happening every day at noon since then. Goes away at one. This is the fourth day, and he was in my office when it happened. Said the bird was on his shoulder, that he could see it and feel it. Nothing there. Is he nuts?"

He didn't answer for a moment, then he said, "The way you describe it, the thing sounds like a posthypnotic suggestion."

"A what?"

"Posthypnotic suggestion. You know, hypnosis."

I groaned. The little I knew about hypnotism supported that explanation. I said, "Would it work, Bruce? I mean, would it be that real to him?"

"Under the right conditions. Wouldn't work with everybody, but a lot of people can get positive visual hallucinations as a result of hypnosis."

"Don't go away," I said. "I'll be right down."

I hung up, put the bill of sale making me "owner" of Weather's back in its envelope and locked it in the middle drawer of my desk. Then I took off.

Bruce Wilson was a tall, bony man with a thick shock of brown hair, and alert brown eyes sparkling over sharp cheekbones. He leaned back in the chair behind his paper-littered desk, looped his left leg over the chair arm and said, speaking as slowly as he always did, "What's a private dick doing with a vanishing parrot?"

"Just walked in on me, Bruce. There's more that's funny, but the parrot business really puzzles me. Never ran across anything like it before. Spell out that hypnosis angle for me, will you?"

He reached up and squeezed his chin. "Simple enough. If a good hypnotic subject, one capable of experiencing positive visual hallucinations, is told while under hypnosis that he'll see a parrot after he's awakened—or at a certain time of day—he'll see it. Doesn't have to be a parrot, of course; could be a monkey, dog, woman, platypus—anything at all that the subject has seen before." He paused. "You ever see a guy with delirium tremens?"

"DT's? Yeah. Wino in Pedro."

"What happened?"

"I woke him up in the middle of the night and the guy started raving. He'd had some flying lessons once, and thought he was coming in for a landing. Then he began seeing spiders on his arms. Started batting at the things . . ." I finally got what Bruce was driving at.

"Uh-huh," Bruce said. "But there weren't any spiders, naturally. He saw them, though, just as this friend of yours sees the parrot."

"Yeah, but . . ."

Bruce held up a yellow pencil in his right hand. "See this?"

"Sure I see it."

"All right, here's what's happening. When light hits the retina it trips a trigger, so to speak, that shoots an impulse along nerve pathways to your brain, and you get a picture in your brain of a pencil—in other words, a nerve pattern up there in your head that lets you see this pencil. The pencil, itself, is merely the means of tripping that trigger and forming the pattern in your brain. If you remove the pencil, yet still tripped that particular trigger—stimulated the same nerve pathways and formed the same nerve patterns in your brain—then you'd still see the pencil.

"The point is, we don't really see with our eyes; they're just the windows. We actually see with our brains, so trip the right trigger and you see the spider or whatever again. Your wino in Pedro did it unintentionally by the combination of liquor, lack of proper food, vitamins, and rest. But the spiders were real to him. Just as real as the voices were to Saint Joan of Arc, or the Lady was to Saint Bernadette. Or the parrot to your friend. What I'm getting at is that the same thing can be done with hypnosis."

I squinted at Bruce. "To anybody? Me, for example?"

"No." He shook his head. "Just about everybody's susceptible to hypnosis in some degree, but visual hallucinations require a deep trance and, usually, only about two out of five average subjects are able to cooperate that completely."

He smiled slightly. "And I guess it's just as well, because we're stuck with minor forms of hypnotic suggestion every day of our lives: radio commercials, advertising, political propaganda. When you get right down to it, all our prejudices, including the racial ones, are little more than conditioned reflexes. A good hypnotist can make you brush your teeth with soap, or believe a Communist prison camp is Utopia, or love your neighbor."

"Yeah. This deep-trance business, Bruce. What do you mean, cooperate?"

"Just that. Except when drugs are used or the subject has been previously conditioned, the success of any hypnosis is primarily up to the subject. Normally he has to cooperate with the hypnotist. Of course I'm talking about the usual clinical technique when both subject and therapist have the same end in mind. There are indirect techniques, and drugs have been used with marked success." He leaned back in his chair and propped his feet on the desk. "That about what you wanted?"

I grinned at him. He was getting there, and as usual he was taking the long way around. When a guy's been making his money from the investigation of crime and criminals for several years, as I have, unless he's completely bald inside his head he's bound to start wondering why some of the characters who steal and kill get that way. I'd started wondering, and that's how I'd got to know Bruce Wilson.

For three years now, I'd been dropping in occasionally to say hello. Usually I wound up spending the day with him if I wasn't on a case, listening to him jaw or jawing myself. And always he took the long way around. I had an idea he just liked to hear himself talk.

"Okay," I said. "You think that's the trouble with my friend?"

"I didn't say that at all. I'd have to talk to him. But from what you said, it sounds as if it might well be that. You mentioned the hallucination occurs every day at the same time, lasts an hour, then disappears. Sounds like it."

"Suppose this bird is a posthypnotic suggestion. Assume that's it. Why the hell didn't Jay tell me he'd been hypnotized?"

He shook his head. "I thought you knew better than that. Don't you suppose a power that would cause a man to see a nonexistent animal could also make him forget he was ever hypnotized? As a matter of fact, when the subject's been in a deep trance there's usually no memory of the hypnosis at all. Posthypnotic amnesia it's called, and it's common. In any event, if the subject's in a deep trance, the operator or therapist—hypnotist if you want to use the slightly discredited word—can always remove memory of it. All he has to do is tell the subject he won't remember and that memory is erased from the conscious mind just as easily as words are erased from the tape of a recorder."

"Wait a minute," I said. "You mean it's possible that could have happened to my friend?"

"It's possible. And he wouldn't remember anything about it. The suggestions would take effect, and naturally he'd be puzzled if the suggestions were bizarre ones. If they were simple, normal things he'd probably carry out the suggestions without even thinking twice about them. If anybody asked him why he was doing that particular thing he'd probably make up a logical reason, one which he'd believe himself."

"I'll be damned. It's a little hard to believe." Suddenly a thought hit me. "Good Lord, Bruce. If a guy could be hypnotized, then told to forget all about it . . ." I stopped. Bruce was smiling.

"Exactly," he said. He pulled his feet off the desk, scooted his chair forward and leaned on the desk top. "Once those particular manifestations of hypnosis sink in, that's a thought you're bound to come up with. Strange feeling, isn't it, to know that it's within the bounds of possibility that you, yourself, might have been hypnotized once or several times? Yesterday, last week, last year—today, even. Only you don't remember it. It could have happened to anybody. Anybody on God's green earth. And they wouldn't know a thing about it. It's conceivable that some of the things you've done were posthypnotic suggestions which you carried out even while you were rationalizing them as logical behavior."

"But that's silly," I said. "Hell, I know I've never been hypnotized. Why, that's . . ." I stopped talking. The idea was frightening.

Bruce kept grinning. "Well, don't get excited about it. It is a possibility, of course, but it's not very probable. Except under certain conditions, the active cooperation of the subject has to be obtained—and there are very few people who'd keep such knowledge from the person who'd been hypnotized. There'd be no point in it, and it might cause serious mental conflict and even derangement. Want some more?"

I stubbed out my cigarette, thinking of Jay's pinched face. "What do you mean, except under certain conditions?"

"Oh, indirect techniques of hypnosis. They're all through the literature; recent experiments. And, too, we're developing the use of drugs in hypnosis—narcohypnosis. Lot of that during the war."

"Drugs?"

"Sure. Sodium Pentothal, for instance. Or Amytal. The drugs lower the subject's resistance; they're cortical depressants and their use makes the inhibitory centers less active—sort of paves the way to the subconscious mind and makes hypnosis much easier. Usually they're injected into the vein on the back of the hand or here at the crook of the arm." He tapped the inside of his arm at the elbow.

I shook my head. "Wow. I came in to ask you about a parrot. But, maybe that's the answer, huh? Posthypnotic suggestion?"

"It's possible. Might be something else, but the description dovetails neatly. It sounds as if this friend of yours might have been given suggestions in a hypnotic trance by someone—somebody showing off, probably—and then the suggestions weren't removed from his mind. Sounds like a serious mistake by a dangerous damned amateur playing around with something he knows nothing about."

I got up. "That's plenty for one day."

He grinned up at me. "Just a minute." He got to his feet and walked to a bookcase, took out a couple volumes and brought them back. He handed them to me and said, "These'll bring you a little more up to date, if you're interested. And let me know what happens with your friend. Bring him here if you want to."

"Good deal, Bruce. I'll drop in tomorrow. If he's game, I'll bring him along with me."

He nodded and I left. It was three o'clock in the afternoon, and I headed for the office. I had an hour and a half to kill before I went down to see Jay at his store, and I figured I'd spend the time reading the books Bruce had given me. Might be I'd find out something else Jay would be glad to know about.

Besides, I wanted to know more about this thing that could make a man see a parrot that didn't exist—this thing that might, conceivably, have happened to anyone.

4

At four-thirty i closed one of the books on hypnosis and shoved my chair back from the desk. My mind was spinning. I'd seldom run across anything so fraught with possibilities for good and opportunity for evil in my life.

I took my .357 Magnum out of the desk, strapped the spring shoulder holster on and checked the gun's cylinder. I looked at the five lethal cartridges thinking they were simply one other way, more direct and less subtle, of making men do what you wanted.

I stuffed the gun in its holster and went out.

Jay Weather was alone when I walked into the big store on Ninth Street. I felt ill at ease when I saw him, but I made myself act as if I felt normal. I walked in past a long row of suits and he nodded at me.

"Hello, Mark." He glanced at his watch. "Got about ten minutes—if they're on time."

I grinned at him and said lightly, "The faithful employee. I'm doubling your salary, Jay."

He smiled a little, but seemed preoccupied. "What'll we say to them?" he asked.

"I dunno. Just tell the guys there's no business. New owner—me. Probably they'll retire in good order."

A frown creased his forehead. "Afraid not. I've been—you know—not thinking too clearly, but these fellows are funny. Don't act like they'll take no for an answer."

"They'll have to. Sounds as if it might be a couple of tough boys trying to muscle in on your business—new gimmick on the old protection racket. Anyway, you probably won't see them again after today."

"I wish I could believe that. I don't think they'll like this."

"Who the hell cares if they like it or not?" I added casually. "By the way, I think I know where that big green parrot of yours came from."

"Huh? What do you mean?"

"I talked to a psychiatrist a couple of hours ago." He flinched, but I went on, "He thinks it might be a case of posthypnotic suggestion."

"Of what?"

"Hypnotism. Suggestions given under hypnosis."

He smiled and shook his head. "Can't buy that."

"Why? Don't you remember ever being hypnotized?"

"Oh, yeah, once. But I gave a speech, is all. Didn't have anything to do with a damn parrot."

I said, "You wouldn't necessarily remember it, Jay. Believe me, I'm serious."

He bit his lip. "Well . . ." Then he glanced up. "Here they come."

I looked toward the entrance. Two men, both husky, solid-looking guys, had come in and were walking toward us. One was about six-one with wide shoulders in a brown tweed coat. The other man was about two inches shorter and maybe twenty pounds lighter. The bigger man had a long, hooked nose in a heavy face. I wouldn't have looked twice at the second man if I'd met him on the street. The shorter of the two stopped a few feet from us and leaned on a glass showcase. The taller man walked up to Jay and me.

"Afternoon, Mr. Weather. We're right on time, you see." He spoke clearly and distinctly, with the too-precise inflection of a would-be radio announcer. He ignored me and said to Jay, "I can have the twenty-five thousand here fifteen minutes after you say the word. I hope you've made up your mind."

It shocked me a little. Up to this point I'd been inclined to regard Jay's story about two guys trying to buy the business for a song as exaggerated. But here it was.

Jay shook his head. "No. I told you I didn't intend to sell to you. I don't know what you're after, but I wish you'd leave—"

"Oh, come now. After all—" The big guy broke off and glanced at me. I'd been standing about three feet away from him, looking him over.

"You," he said. "Run along."

I smiled at him.

He frowned, then shrugged his shoulders slightly and shifted his feet a little so he faced me. He grinned back, pleasantly, flesh bunching at the corners of his mouth. "You didn't hear me at all," he said quietly. "This is private. Take a walk."

"Uh-uh."

He stopped smiling and took a step toward me. He balled his left hand into a formidable fist, placed it gently on my chest, and shoved. I went back half a step and his eyes got a puzzled look. I figured he'd felt the strap of the shoulder harness that held my gun. His eyes flicked to my left armpit, then back to my face. Then his lip curled and he turned his head slowly and stared at Jay.

Jay said hesitantly, as if he were wondering if this had been such a good idea after all, "Mr. Lucian, this is Mr. Logan. He's the new owner of Weather's."

Lucian frowned and looked at me again as Jay went on, "This noon I went to Mr. Logan's office and sold him the business. It's his. I don't have anything to do with it anymore. You'll have to talk to him."

I said, "That's right, Lucian. I'm the boss now. I'm in no mood for any more business talk today, or any day. Sell you a suit, though."

Lucian's jaw sagged an eighth of an inch and he gawked at me.

"Good-by," I said.

His face flushed and suddenly he reached out with his left hand, grabbed Jay by the front of his shirt and pulled him close. "Listen, bum," he began, but I stopped him.

I chopped at the base of his upper arm with the edge of my open hand. I didn't swing very hard, but it doesn't take much, and his fingers slipped from Jay's shirt. He grunted and wiggled his hand a couple times, opening and closing it; then he turned toward me.

I glanced at the other guy, standing erect now by the showcase, then stepped up close to Lucian. I said, "Look, mister. You've thrown your weight around enough. Beat it, and don't come back. I don't know what your angle is, but it's no good now."

He looked into my face and breathed, "You son of a bitch." I could smell garlic on his breath. The corners of his mouth were twisted downward. Moving so fast he caught me flat-footed, he slammed his open right hand hard into my chest again. I staggered back, stumbled and caught myself, then stood where I was, four or five feet from Jay and Lucian.

That settled it. When they'd first come in, all I'd wanted was to convince the boys there'd be no business done today or any other day. Now it was different. My heart was slamming at my chest and I could feel the muscles in my arms starting to tighten. I made myself relax, and peeled open the fists

I'd made of my hands, as Lucian started toward me. The guy was damned sure of himself.

The other man had laughed loudly when I stumbled backward, but he didn't make a move toward us. He was lounging on the glass counter again as if there weren't a chance Lucian might need any help with just me.

I said, "That was a mistake, mister."

Lucian grinned and kept coming toward me, moving gracefully, with all the confidence in the world; it was a safe bet he knew how to handle himself. He was poised, ready to block anything I might throw at him. So I waited for him.

The trouble with most tough boys is that they think the only way to take care of a guy is to hit him so hard he loses interest in everything. They're used to nice, clean little fighting men who adhere reasonably close to the Marquis of Queensberry rules. So the tough boy knocks the gentleman down, and then kicks him in the mouth. I wouldn't still be alive if I were that nice or that stupid.

Lucian stepped up closer. He didn't swing, but kept his eyes on my face and reached out with his right hand again. I guess he didn't expect me to do anything but let him shove me around, because he placed his open hand on my chest, grinning happily. I didn't stop him, but when he touched my chest, I reached up with my left hand, dug my thumb between his middle and second fingers and grabbed the second and little fingers tight. I squeezed just as he shoved. I went back on my right foot, but as I moved I jerked his palm upward, then twisted my wrist a quarter turn to the right, bending his two fingers back the wrong way.

I knew what was going to happen—and all of a sudden so did Lucian. That two-finger routine is elementary judo, called familiarly a "come-along," and it looks like nothing until it happens to you. Lucian's eyes got wide just before the pain hit him and lanced up his wrist, then he sucked in his breath sharply, noise squeaking in his throat. He went up on his toes and leaned slightly forward, his lips pulled back and his mouth opened so wide I could see dark fillings in his lower teeth.

I pulled gently, twisting down on his fingers, and he took two mincing steps forward while I turned easily and let him walk around me on tiptoe. To somebody fifty feet away, we would have looked like two fairies dancing in slow motion, but Lucian was completely helpless. He couldn't swing his free left hand at me because another breath of pressure would have squeezed him down on his knees. Another ounce would have broken his fingers.

And I barely kept myself from snapping my wrist and shoving the white bones of his fingers out through the taut skin. I still had a burn inside me, and somebody was going to have to teach this boy some day. But I stopped just in time and eased off on the pressure a little bit.

Lucian hadn't been able to get a word out past the pain, and as I eased off he gasped, "Stop it; Christ, stop it."

"You gonna leave? Keep the hell away from this place?"

I didn't catch his answer, if there was one. Those two or three mincing steps he'd taken had turned me almost halfway around, and I'd been so griped at him that I'd paid too little attention to the other smart boy. He paid a lot of attention to me, though, and he paid it all on the back of my head.

When I came to, Jay was patting my face with a cold rag that dripped water. I was flat on my back and my eyes didn't focus right away. Finally the haze up above me turned into a ceiling and I groaned and said the only thing that seemed appropriate: "Son of a bitch. What happened?"

Jay sighed with relief. "You been out ten minutes," he said. "The other guy hit you on the head with a gun."

I could have guessed it was something like that. I sat up, and the way the back of my head felt, I wondered if I'd left a chunk of it on the floor. I was almost afraid to look. There was a small red spot on the thick carpet, and the back of my head was sticky when I felt it.

"They gone?" I asked.

"Yeah. Told me to keep my mouth shut, then searched you and left."

I saw my wallet, papers, and loose change on the floor near me. "Damn it," I said. "What'd they do, clean me out?" The way my head hurt, I didn't really care. I picked up the wallet and looked inside. Everything was there: photostat of my detective's license, driver's license, the rest of my cards and papers. And almost three hundred and fifty dollars in bills. I gathered up my stuff and put it back in my pockets, then got to my feet and waited till the dizziness went away.

"Why the devil did they search me, Jay?"

"Don't know. They left right after that."

Suddenly I thought of something. "Look. You go on home and I'll come over in an hour or so. Okay? I think I can convince you about that hypnosis business."

"All right, Mark. Where are you going?"

"Just a hunch. Those boys searched me, so they know who I am." I grabbed for my gun. It was still there, so apparently the guys had been content just to bat my skull. "Something I want to check."

Jay nodded and I went out. I was still thinking about my having been searched. Maybe Lucian and his pal hadn't swallowed the story that I was the

21

new owner of Weather's. Or, if they had, they might have begun to wonder whether I had a bill of sale. I hotfooted it for the Farnsworth Building.

I could have taken my time. The office door was ajar; its lock had been forced. Nothing was disturbed inside the office except the desk. Two side drawers and the center drawer had been broken into. The bill of sale that Jay and I had signed earlier was gone.

5

Except for a headache, I was in pretty good shape, so I finished my dinner, had coffee and a cigarette, and headed for Jay's, hoping Gladys wouldn't throw a fit when she saw me. It was seven o'clock and dark now.

Gladys opened the door and glared at me. She didn't look surprised, just angry. Apparently Jay had mentioned I was coming by and she'd had time to work up to a fury.

"Hello, Mrs. Weather," I said.

"You fool!" she hissed softly. "You've got your nerve. What do you mean by that talk about—"

I interrupted just as softly, but more pleasantly, "Look, Gladys, we don't even know each other. Let's leave it that way. Are you going to invite me in?"

"I'll invite you to hell," she said, but she swung the door wider and I brushed past her. The familiar scent of her body climbed up into my nostrils, and my stomach felt hollow for a moment, but I went on into the living room. Jay had spent a sizable chunk for his big home here on St. Andrews Place. It had two stories and sixteen rooms, all tastefully and expensively furnished. I walked across a deep carpet to a long divan and sat down at one end of it. Gladys sat at the other end and turned toward me.

Finally she said, "You're really serious, aren't you?" Both her voice and expression showed her contempt. Contempt for me, I suppose, because I let a little thing like a husband bother me.

I said, "You know I'm serious. Look, you knew this was going to happen sooner or later. I told you as much at least half a dozen times. And this afternoon I told you why."

She let her dark eyes rest on me for a moment, then shrugged. She didn't say anything.

I said, "You like to think of yourself as adult and modern—not Victorian, at least—so let's be adult for a minute and talk sensibly about Jay. Has he seemed all right lately?"

"Of course he's all right."

"I mean, has he seemed more worried than usual? Maybe acted a little odd?"

She shook her head, dark hair swinging, and I remembered it tangled against my pillow. "He's the same as always," she said.

"Incidentally, where is he?"

"Upstairs in the tub. Drowning, possibly."

"Ah, you're a lovely girl, Gladys. Tell me, has Jay said anything about a parrot?"

"No. Why would he?" She looked puzzled.

I started to answer her when the front door slammed and somebody came into the living room. I heard a girl's voice say, "Oh, I'm sorry, Gladys," and I looked up.

She was a little blond gal, five-three or so, right out of the bandbox in a bright green wool sweater and skirt. She looked pretty enough to preserve in marble, and her hair was piled high on top of her head in a complicated swirl.

She came right in and Gladys said, after a long pause, "I think you used to know Mr. Logan, didn't you, Ann, dear?"

Was this the little beast that used to bedevil me? Ann Weather, Jay's daughter by his first marriage? I stood up and shook my head a little. I guess no man ever gets used to the things that happen to little girls when they grow up. He gets used to the things, maybe, but never the transformation. Little boys grow up and become men, but it seems like they simply get bigger and a bit uglier, maybe. Little girls, though—that's different. They not only get bigger, but they grow in a hell of a lot of different directions. Ann had grown right in all the right directions.

She walked gracefully across the room toward me and held out her hand. "Of course, Mr. Logan. Mark, isn't it? I didn't recognize you at first."

I grinned down at her. "I'll bet you still don't. Probably repressed the memory. Last time I saw you, you were pretty disgusting."

She looked shocked, her head cocked to one side.

"You were about ten or eleven," I said. "You kicked me in the shin."

She put her head down and laughed, all the while looking up at me from under long lashes she was probably proud of. "I do remember you, though. I even remember kicking you. Besides, I've seen your picture in the newspapers with stories about guns and things."

I said, inadequately, "You've changed, Miss Weather."

Still looking steadily up at me she said slowly, "I know I have—more than you realize. Call me Ann, Mark."

She sat down in an easy chair and I sank back onto the divan. Looking at Ann, I said, "We were talking about Jay. I saw him earlier and he seemed a little worn out—you know, nervous and sort of jumpy. Has anything happened recently to upset him?"

Gladys slowly shook her head. "I don't think so. We had a nice enough weekend."

Ann chimed in, "Yes, we had a wonderful party Saturday night. You should have been here, Mark."

"Wish I had been. Big deal?"

"Just the three of us and two other couples," Gladys said. "And Ann's boyfriend."

Ann snorted. "Boyfriend! He's a year younger than I am. Gladys's idea of a nice boy for me." She looked at Gladys and said, "That one didn't take at all. I'll bet he wears long underwear." She laughed softly and said, "I liked the hypnotist a lot better."

I opened my mouth, then shut it slowly. Ann sat deep in the overstuffed chair, her legs extended straight out in front of her, her arms resting on the arms of the chair. The wool sweater and skirt rested against her body the way wool always does.

Ann asked, "Do you believe in hypnotism, Mark?"

"Yeah, I believe in it."

She blinked at me. "What's the matter? You look funny."

"I always look funny."

She laughed and said, "That's not what I meant, and you don't look funny, either. I mean you looked surprised."

"Guess I was," I said. "You don't run across a hypnotist at a party every day. How did Jay act when he was hypnotized?"

Gladys said, "I'm not too clear about that—"

"He gave a speech," Ann interrupted. "Darn good one, too."

I looked pleasantly at Gladys. "You say you're not clear about what went on, Mrs. Weather?"

"No, I'm not. I was one of the subjects, too. I'm told I was—amusing."

"Told? Don't you remember?"

She shook her head. "I remember almost nothing about the party. I'm afraid I can't tell you anything."

"Were you and Jay the only ones hypnotized?"

"No," Gladys said. "One of our acquaintances, a girl named Ayla Veichek. Just the three of us."

"That's all," Ann broke in. "Wouldn't work with me." She laughed softly and stared at me. "I was a little scared. I was afraid he might . . ." She let her voice trail off, but she was smiling slightly.

A horrible sound floated down from upstairs. The words were "Home on the Range," but the tune was a new one. I grinned at Gladys and asked her, "Does Jay always murder songs like that?"

She smiled. "Isn't it awful? I'm afraid he does, but we're used to it. He'll be down in a minute."

"Gladys. Hey, Gladys," Jay was yelling from upstairs.

Gladys sighed. "Excuse me a minute. He probably can't find his shoes or something." She laughed slightly, the corners of her mouth pulling down as she glanced at me, then she got up and went out.

Almost immediately Ann said, "Mark, how long are you going to be here?"

"Oh, half an hour or so, probably. Why?"

She spoke softly. "I want to talk to you. When you leave, how about stopping at Frankie's on Beverly?"

"Frankie's? Isn't that a cocktail lounge?"

"That's the place. And don't look so stupefied; I'm twenty-one. Don't I look it?" She was smiling.

I grinned at her. "You're just a baby."

She stopped smiling, slowly, but she didn't act at all irritated. I noted her lips were plump and smooth, protruding a little now as she lowered her chin, mouth closed, and sucked in her cheeks, making little hollows that accentuated her rather high cheekbones. It was a calculated little movement, and she looked good, and she knew she looked good.

She breathed in deeply and said slowly, "All right. Call me baby."

I said to myself, God damn! Then Gladys came back in before I could ask Ann what she wanted to talk to me about. I think that's what I was going to ask her.

Gladys said, "He'll be right down, Mr. Logan."

"What? Who?"

Mrs. Weather looked at me strangely and said, "Why, Jay," and Ann threw back her head and burst into laughter. She laughed, and while she laughed, she wriggled.

I wriggled a little, too. I could feel a slow flush coming up my neck and creeping over my face.

Ann's eyes were still on me, and she looked for a moment like one of the old-time movie sirens getting ready to seduce the hero. Then a giggle squeaked out of her and she burst into laughter again.

She was a cute kid. Be easy to strangle her.

"My word," said Mrs. Weather. "What's going on?"

I smiled a small smile. "Ann's second childhood, I guess."

"Second childhood? Why, she's still not out of her first one."

Ann stopped laughing and glared at Mrs. Weather, but Gladys couldn't really have meant it. If she did, she still had a lot to learn about her stepdaughter. Maybe I did too.

Jay came in just then and said, "Hello, Mark. How's the head?"

"Pretty good. I'd forgotten about it."

Ann said, "Forgotten your head?" As I turned to look at her I saw her mouth open. Apparently she'd just noticed the patch at the back of my skull. She got up and walked over to me.

"My gosh," she said. "I hadn't noticed that before. What happened?"

"A guy hit me on the head."

"Does it hurt?"

"No," I said. "It's okay now."

She said, "I know why I didn't see it before. I couldn't see the back of your head because you were always looking at me." She'd been gently touching the patch and she let her hand trail off and whisper across the nape of my neck.

"Damn fool girl," Jay said to me. "Thinks she's Mata Hari." But his voice was warm and he smiled at her. "She oughta be spanked," he added.

Ann turned around and walked slowly back to her chair. As she turned I chose that moment to look, being me. She did need a spanking, and she was pretty much of a pain, and the thought of spanking her wasn't a revolting idea at all.

Jay said, "You mean you've been here all this time and nobody's fixed you a drink? Come on, Mark."

He'd hit it right on the head: I needed a drink. I followed Jay through a couple of big rooms and into a den at the back of the house. The den was Jay's pride, and he'd fixed it up well, but it was more bar than den. Against the right wall was a completely equipped home bar with glass top, and four bamboo stools. I perched on the end stool while Jay began mixing a Coke-high for himself and a rum and soda for me.

I asked, "Jay, haven't you said anything at all to Gladys and Ann about the parrot? Or about the business deal?"

He shook his head. "Uh-uh. Afraid . . . you know, afraid they'd figure I was nuts or something."

"Believe me, Jay, I'm positive it's nothing like that."

He smiled a little. "Hypnotism again?"

"What about the hypnotist who was here Saturday night?"

"Oh, that," he said.

It surprised me a little bit. I'd been expecting him to say, "What hypnotist?" He went on, "I been thinking since I saw you and I figured that might get you. There was one here, all right, but it was just a party. Had some friends in. No parrot. It can't have any connection."

"The hell. You remember what you did?"

"Well, not exactly. Gladys and Ann have been kidding me about it a little. Seems I made a big speech."

"Uh-huh. Listen to this—a man can be hypnotized and told he won't remember anything about what he did, and he won't remember. Isn't it worth checking?"

He looked at me for several seconds. Then he nodded slowly. "Maybe you're the crazy one, but I guess so."

He stirred the liquor gently with a swizzle stick and handed me my drink. I had a swallow, then said, "How about doing me a personal favor? Come down tomorrow and talk to that psychiatrist friend of mine." I added quickly, "I mean so he can explain the hypnosis angle I've been trying to pound into your head. Maybe he can get rid of your bird."

He shrugged his thin shoulders. "Okay, Mark. Come on, let's go back."

"One other thing, Jay. Do you mind if we go over this deal with your wife and daughter? There's something screwy going on. Besides, it might do you good to get it off your chest."

He pursed his lips. "Well, let's let it out for tonight," he said. "Wait till I see that brain doctor."

I let it go. I decided not to say anything to him about the theft of the bill of sale, because it seemed to me he had enough on his mind for now. There was little point in giving him more worries. I grabbed my drink and followed him back into the living room.

When we went in I noticed Ann wasn't in sight. Gladys still sat on the divan and I asked her, "Did Ann take off?"

"Yes. She's always in and out, going or coming."

If Ann had gone ahead to Frankie's, she must have been pretty sure I'd meet her. She hadn't done anything to make me think she wasn't pretty sure of herself. I sat down in the chair and Jay joined his wife on the divan. There is no room so crowded as one that contains a woman, her husband, and her lover, and for five minutes conversation was strained. Then Jay asked me if I felt like playing a game of chess.

"Guess not, Jay. I'll beat it pretty quick." I turned to Gladys. "Say, this hypnotist. He an amateur?"

"No," she said. "He's a professional; that's his business. He has an office downtown."

"Could you give me his name and address?"

"Why, certainly, Mr. Logan. His name is Borden, Joseph Borden, and his office is in the Langer Building on Olive."

Jay looked at me and shook his head as if he were trying to tell me again that I was barking up the wrong tree.

I glanced at my watch. It was five after eight, and if Ann were at Frankie's she might be getting impatient.

"Thanks," I said. "Think I'll take off. See you tomorrow then, Jay?"

He nodded and got up. As I left him at the door I said, "Bet you five you don't have any more trouble after tomorrow."

I didn't know how right I was.

6

Frankie's was a small place with pleasantly dim lighting, and table service only—no bar or stools. Drinks were brought from some place in back. Tables filled the center area of the club, and plush, black-leather booths lined all four sides of the room.

A slim young man played, almost idly, on a piano surrounded by tables in the middle of the room, and every few minutes he'd sing. At least he was billed as the singer, though he might well have been called the chanteuse. The songs consisted mainly of his breathing delicately into the microphone a few inches from his expressive face. Once in a while you could catch a word like *amour*, but the real thrills were the gasps and sighs and moans. He was sexy.

I'd never been in here before and I paused inside the entrance, until I saw a white handkerchief being waved back and forth above a blond head at a booth in a far corner. I nodded at a tall, slim chappie who danced up, then walked by him and to the booth.

Ann's green eyes twinkled and she patted the black leather cushion at her side. I said, "Hello, baby," and sat down opposite her with the small round table between us.

"Hello," she said, then got up, marched around to my side of the booth and squeezed in beside me. "You took your time."

"I'm here. Almost didn't come."

She laughed delightedly. "I'll bet. I'll just bet."

"Why here, of all places?" I asked her.

"Here you'll really appreciate me, Mark." She was all of a foot away from me, and she locked her hands behind her head, arching her back, looking at me. "You do appreciate me, don't you, Mark?"

"Sure, child. Let's get down to business."

She unclasped her hands, wrapped her arms around my neck, and pulled herself to me. "All right," she said softly just before she kissed me on the lips.

It jarred me. Maybe I shouldn't have been so surprised, but I was, and my eyes were wide open as she leaned forward and pressed her lips on mine. The long brown lashes fluttered softly an inch from my eyes, then she opened her eyes and looked at me steadily as her plump, smooth lips moved gently, with a practiced expertness. For just a moment she was content and serious, then her lids crinkled and I could feel her mouth smiling under mine.

I reached up automatically and pushed her away from me. Out of my mind, I guess.

She said, "Fresh," and looked down at my hands.

I dropped them quickly and said, "Woman, what are you trying to prove?"

"Woman." She smiled. "That's better. And I'm not trying to prove anything. I wanted to kiss you."

"So you kissed me. This is hardly the place." I sounded stuffy.

She grinned. "Oh? Where would you like to be kissed? Anyway, this is a perfect place. A woman could be raped in here and not a soul would notice the woman."

I had to grin at the little witch. "Tell me, Ann. Did you really want to talk to me, or is this some kind of psychological experiment?"

"It's an experiment. Not psychological, though. And I did want to talk to you. First I was going to lure you here, and if I needed an excuse I was going to tell you it was because Gladys was lying to you."

"Lying?" I couldn't figure this girl. She'd reeled that out as if it were nothing. "You need an excuse," I told her. "Lying about what?"

"You're some date," she said. "Aren't you going to buy me a drink?"

"I'm not a date, but I'll buy you a drink."

"I'll have a French Seventy-five. What'll you have? Acid?"

I ignored her and caught our waiter's eye. I gave him the order and when he'd left I looked at Ann. "Spill. What did Gladys lie to me about?"

Conversation had stopped while I got the waiter and ordered and I hadn't been watching Ann. Now I noticed that she was staring at me, not just looking, but staring with an odd kind of intentness at my lips, and her own lips were pressed tightly together. She didn't look cute, as she had before; she looked older and, somehow, more mature, almost animal. Ann looked very much as Gladys had sometimes looked. I had to repeat my question.

She blinked twice, slowly, then smiled. "I'm sorry, Mark. I was somewhere else, I guess. Gladys—she said she didn't remember what went on at the party."

"And she did."

"Of course she did. We talked about the party for an hour or more on Monday, and we both kidded Dad when he came home Monday night."

"What did he do?"

"Mr. Borden told him he was Hitler and had to make a speech, and he did it up brown. Funny thing. Dad had German in college but hadn't used it since. He gave the whole speech in fluent German. Isn't that funny?"

"Yeah." Ann's conversation was animated again, but she was pressed close to me in the wide booth and I could feel the tips of her fingers resting, perhaps by accident, against my thigh. I swallowed, "You don't like Mrs. Weather much, do you?"

"Why do you ask that?"

"Simple. You drag me here and tell me she was lying."

She smiled. "I don't like her. And I didn't drag you here; you came running. And I got you here, didn't I?"

"But not for long. Has Jay seemed worried lately? Out of sorts?"

"Uh-huh. Something on his mind. Don't know what, but I could tell he's been worried."

"Gladys hadn't noticed."

"Or so she said. Anyway, she wouldn't notice if the moon fell down."

I sat quietly for a moment thinking about Jay and his damned parrot. He hadn't seemed to like the idea of spilling that story to his family, and hadn't believed me at first—maybe still didn't—when I'd told him I was convinced it was the result of hypnotism. I didn't like to see Jay going to pieces the way he was, and I meant to run his elusive bird down for a lot of reasons. Friendship and his trust in me and belief that I could help him; Gladys, too, of course. It seemed to me that I owed Jay a lot more now than I could pay back. But I couldn't help him much by keeping my mouth shut, and there were some screwy angles to this mess. I thought about it a minute longer, then gave Ann the story of Jay's parrot. I wound up saying, "So that's it. I'll see that guy Borden tonight if I can find him. Something smells."

She was completely serious and frowning now. "I didn't know anything about that, Mark. I know Dad's been worried this last week, but I figured it'd pass. Funny, there wasn't anything at the party about a parrot. Just some tricks like that Hitler thing, and a hypnosis lecture Borden gave."

"What sort of tricks? What else did he have Jay do? Tell me the whole story, will you?"

The waiter brought the drinks and I swallowed at my rum and soda while Ann talked. "We had dinner Saturday night—eight of us—and Borden showed up at eight o'clock. He gave a lecture, then demonstrated a falling routine with Dad—you know, where he'd stand up and Borden would say he was falling backward, falling back, back, and so on, then Dad fell and Borden caught him. He did a few more things with Dad, demonstrations like hypnopendulum, arm heaviness, and so on."

I interrupted. "You seem to know quite a lot about this. How come?"

"I was a psychology major in college. I still read the *Journal of General Psychology* and some of the others."

"Still?"

She smiled and said matter-of-factly, "I graduated top of my class over a year ago. I'm a brain. Really. I guess I'm practically a genius." She laughed.

"Last year? But you're only twenty-one now."

"Oh!" she said, exasperated. "*Only* twenty-one. If I'd started using heroin when I was fifteen, how old would I be now?" She tossed her head. "Anyway, when Borden finished that stuff he made us all relax and then attempted group hypnosis. Good results with Dad, Gladys, and Ayla. Then he took them one at a time and hypnotized them. He didn't leave till after midnight. Lots of fun, but it didn't work on me. I suppose it's my fault. I wanted to see what went on. Besides, I didn't want him to hypnotize me." She stopped and looked at me, sucking in her cheeks a little. Then she said mischievously, "I'd let you if you wanted to, Mark."

I ignored her and said, "And then what?"

"Why, I'd be completely in your power, darling."

"Damn it, you know what I meant. And then what happened at the party?"

She was looking at my mouth again, her cheeks still sucked in a little and her closed mouth moving gently as if she were biting easily on the insides of her cheeks. Her lips slid together, back and forth a fraction of an inch, over and over with a kind of kneading motion. Her fingertips still touched my leg and she slid them forward till her palm rested on my thigh, almost burning, as if it were on my skin.

She said with a new, tighter pitch to her voice, "Forget that party, Mark. Let's talk about this party. Our party."

I was getting more confused by the minute. Ann seemed to have two alternating moods; she'd be bright and pleasant for a little while, apparently perfectly normal, and then she would seem affected, almost afflicted, with a kind of strangeness, or maybe passion. I simply couldn't figure her. Not yet.

"Look, Ann, honey," I said. "This ain't no party. See? Just a pleasant chat, and I need some info. Spill."

She sighed and then smiled a little. "Okay. I guess you're the boss." Listening to her voice, there seemed nothing different about it, nothing strained. But her hand, still on my thigh, was trembling a little and I could feel it in my spine.

She kept talking. "Borden had them all do various things. No parrots, though. He told Gladys that after he waked her, every time he touched his nose she'd stand up, clear her throat, and then sit down. She did, too. When Borden asked her why she was doing that she said she had a kink in her back and was trying to work it out. Isn't it funny the way they'll almost always figure out a reason why they're acting on the posthypnotic suggestion?"

"Sometimes not so funny. No parrot, huh?"

"None."

"Jay ever alone with Borden?"

"Let me see . . . once, I think. I believe he went into the den with Dad for a drink. That was after everything was over, though, and they weren't in there very long. Why?"

"Just curious, Ann. I'm not sure of anything. Nothing else you can tell me?"

"Nothing I can think of. All through?" She grinned.

"No. How about writing down a list of the people who were there?"

She didn't answer for a moment, then her expression changed again; her green eyes narrowed and her tongue flicked over her lips. "I'll have to take my hand away," she said. "You've acted as if you didn't even know it was there, Mark."

I was surprised at how tight my voice was when I answered, "I knew it was there."

She smiled, her teeth pressed together, and her palm brushed against me gently, lingeringly. Then she reached for her bag and took a pencil and scrap of paper from it. There was a cottony taste in my mouth.

Just before she started to write, she glanced up at me from under the long lashes and said softly, "Uh-huh. I guess you did know." Then, casually, she said, "Let's see, there were Dad and Gladys and me, and old long-underwear Arthur. Then Mr. Hannibal, Dad's lawyer—he's sort of a friend of the family, too. He was with Miss Stewart. And Peter Sault and Ayla Veichek. He's an artist and she's a model. You'll like her, I'm afraid." She scribbled on the paper as she talked.

"Why will I like her?"

"Because she's delicious. Don't you like delicious women?"

"Of course, but—"

"I'm delicious, too, but maybe she's more your type. You'd call her sexy, I imagine. Voluptuous-looking; even more than me." She paused and added, "Of course, she's a little stupid."

"Now I know I'll like her. But she might not like me."

Ann pushed the list across the little table to me and said, "If she doesn't, you'll know it." She grinned. "And if she does, you'll know that, too. Only one thing wrong with Ayla. She's top-heavy." She smiled at me and went on, as if she were deliberately trying to stimulate my imagination. "I don't know, though, if you were to see her without any clothes on, you might not agree with me. You might like it."

I couldn't think of anything to say.

She went on, "But you've never met Ayla. Be kind of hard for you to imagine what she'd look like nude." She paused and said more softly, "But you can imagine me, can't you, Mark?"

That was the trouble: I *had* been imagining.

"Try it, Mark," she said. "Look at me and try to imagine it." She leaned back away from me, resting against the side of the booth. "Right now, Mark."

I did look at her, at the soft swell and curve of her body beneath the wool that molded it. Then I remembered Gladys and Jay. I made myself look away from her and said gruffly, "For Christ's sake, Ann, give a guy a chance. Now knock it off and pay attention. What makes you think I'll see this Ayla? Or anyone else?"

She sighed, shrugged, and sat up straight. "Simple," she said finally, her voice a little dull. "You ask Gladys about Dad and the party. You pry me with questions. Then there's Dad's parrot. When you leave me you'll go around talking to everybody who was at the party—maybe to see if I'm lying, or if Gladys is lying. Isn't that right? You're a detective."

"Well—"

"Of course you will. Want to have some fun?"

"Well—"

"When you see Peter Sault tell him you're an artist. Maybe he'll show you his oils." She pointed at the list she'd written. "Names, and all the addresses I knew."

"These oils. They're good?"

"They're a scream. He does nudes."

Nudes? Well, I like nudes. "Good," I said. "I dabble in oils in my spare time, then."

She finished her drink. "More."

"Uh-uh. I've gotta see a hypnotist."

"Really, Mark," she said seriously. "I'd like another drink. I don't want you to go. Please." There was a little catch in her voice.

I looked at her curiously. "What's the matter, Ann? You know I've got work to do, and we can't stay here all night." I grinned at her and looked around. "Certainly not in this place. Kind of a funny place for us to be, isn't it?"

She didn't smile back. She said flatly, "This is a fairy club. I feel at home here."

"You? But you're not—"

She interrupted me. "Not that way, no." She hesitated, then moved closer to me, her thigh pressing mine. She kept her hands folded in her lap and looked at me, unsmiling. I knew, before she spoke again, that she was going to tell me something about herself, and suddenly I didn't want to hear whatever it was.

But Ann looked directly at my mouth again and went on hurriedly, "They're all sick; that's why I feel at home here. See that little man alone in the booth across from us?"

I didn't have to look. I'd noticed the guy because the waiter had made three trips to his table while Ann and I had each had one drink. I nodded.

Ann said, "He's queer, and he doesn't like it. Maybe he feels guilty. So, besides everything else, he's a lush. An alcoholic. He's all right till he takes that first drink, and then he's, well, he's not all right. I'm like him. I'm just like him."

I frowned at her, still puzzled, and she made her meaning clear for me with the touch of her hands again, and the pressure of her body as she moved closer to me.

"Only with me it's not liquor, Mark. It's you."

She was just a little bit of a thing but her actions were so strange that she almost frightened me. And, too, there was a hot urgency about her words and movements that communicated itself to me. She was young, warm, lovely—and I was beginning to think of her more as a woman than as the daughter of my friend.

I'd already become far too involved with the Weather family, and I liked Ann too much now. I didn't want to get more deeply involved than I was.

I said, "We've had our talk, Ann. I'll take you home."

She protested, but followed me when I slid out of the booth and walked to the door. As we left, the pianist ran long white fingers over the keyboard and sighed softly into the microphone.

Ann stayed huddled over on her side of the car, eyes closed, arms crossed over her breasts as if she were hugging herself, all the way to her home. Once I glanced at her and saw her hips writhe slightly, sinuously. Her eyes were still closed and she seemed unaware of me.

But when I parked in front of the big house on St. Andrews Place she put a hand on my arm and slid across the seat to sit close by me. "Mark."

"Yes, Ann?"

"I hoped you were taking me someplace else. Not here. Not home."

"I told you I was going to take you home."

"I know. But I thought . . . Never mind. Look at me, Mark."

She pulled herself against me and her face was so close to mine that I could see nothing except the smooth brow, the big green eyes, the curving red lips. There was a tense expression on her face and her lips were moist and parted.

"Kiss me, Mark." One arm went around my neck. She pulled herself closer to me, bending my head to hers, and pressed her lips against mine. The kiss was sweet and soft, her lips warm and gentle. At first. Then it became demanding, hungry, less a kiss than an invitation. I put my arms around her, pulled her to me, mashing her lips under mine as her tongue came alive in my mouth.

Finally I put my hands on her shoulders and pushed her gently away. "Wait a minute, Ann. This isn't good at all."

"Please, Mark." Her hands were busy and eager and her teeth were pressed tightly together. I could see the pulse of fine muscle at the smooth line of her jaw. Her breath was hot, an inch from my lips.

"Ann, I've got to go—right now. We can't . . . I've got to see Borden."

"Mark. Don't you like me at all? Don't you think I'm pretty?"

I could feel the softness of her shoulders under my fingers. Every few seconds her body trembled convulsively and the movement traveled through my fingers and into my body. "Of course you are," I said. "You're lovely, you're wonderful . . ." I stopped. I couldn't find words to tell her how mixed up I was.

"Then don't be cruel," she said. "I told you in the bar how I feel. Help me, Mark. Help me . . ."

Her arms tightened around me and she pressed against me. Her lips covered mine again. Her fingers trailed over my cheek and across my chest. The fingers curved and I felt her nails bite through the thin cloth of my shirt. I could feel my heart pounding heavily.

Her body was soft, yielding against my hands. Then she fumbled with her sweater, pressed my hand upon her skin. I felt her fingers slide under my shirt and her nails raked my chest. I slid my hand up the smooth skin of her side, cupped the firm, warm breast in my palm. Her lips moved from side to side on my mouth and her breath washed over my face. Her breast seemed to burn my palm as she strained her body forward against me. The softness of her breast blended with the smoothness of her thigh, the liquid clinging of her lips.

"Mark," she whispered softly, "Mark, love me love me love me."

It was like ice water thrown on my flesh.

Suddenly I could remember Gladys saying the same thing, in almost the same way, the whispered phrases running together like one word, hot and twisted and eager, Gladys's body straining while her hands clutched convulsively at my skin. Gladys. Mrs. Weather.

I pushed Ann from me, suddenly, roughly.

She gasped. "Mark!"

"Go into the house, Ann." My voice was strange to me, harsh and almost ugly.

"What's the matter? I don't understand."

"Please, Ann. Go on inside."

"Are you serious?"

"Yes."

I don't know how long she looked at me, her eyes unblinking, her mouth tight. Finally she lowered her head and said softly, "Why, Mark?"

"It's nothing. I don't know."

"Is it something wrong with me?"

"No."

"Then why?"

"I can't tell you. I'm not even sure myself. I'm mixed up. Just—just forget it, Ann."

For several moments she was quiet, then she sighed heavily. "I'll go into the house, Mark, and upstairs to my room. And I'll think about you. Is that what you want?"

"I suppose."

"I'll undress, thinking about you. I'll get naked into bed. And I'll think about you. I'll lie awake. And I'll think about you."

She stopped. I didn't say anything.

Ann didn't speak again. After long seconds she got out of the car and closed the door quietly. I heard her high heels clicking over the cement walk. The front door closed behind her.

I sat in the car for a while, then started the engine and drove downtown.

7

Joseph borden answered my ring. I'd checked by telephone and had told him I was a private detective, but so far he didn't know what I was after.

He was a mild-appearing man of medium height, with wavy brown hair and soft blue eyes, a small mustache and a long narrow nose. He was wearing a brown dressing gown with a gold cord looped around his waist. He stood in the doorway of his Catalina Street apartment and said pleasantly, "You're Mr. Logan?"

"That's right, Mr. Borden."

"Come in, please." He stood aside as I went in, then motioned toward an angular, modern chair that turned out to be surprisingly comfortable when I sat in it. The living room was a series of curves and angles that added up to a pleasing whole. Two large bookcases occupied half of one wall, bright paper jackets on many of the books.

Borden sat down in another angular chair a few feet from me and asked brightly, "What can I do for you, Mr. Logan?"

"You're a professional hypnotist, isn't that right?"

"Yes, I am." He waited for me to go on.

"Would you mind giving me a rough idea of your work, Mr. Borden?"

"Not at all. Primarily I lecture and give public and private demonstrations of hypnosis."

"That's really why I'm here. You gave a demonstration at the home of Mr. and Mrs. Weather last Saturday night, didn't you?"

"Yes, I did. Quite successful, I might add." He smiled pleasantly.

"When you hypnotized Mr. Weather, were positive visual hallucinations part of his posthypnotic suggestions?"

He widened his soft blue eyes. "Why, no. I suggested no visual hallucinations at all. The only demonstrations I made with him were that he'd make a speech as Hitler, and then there was one last suggestion toward the end of the evening. When I snapped my fingers he was to say, 'Let's have a nightcap.'" Borden smiled gently. "Rather an interesting way of bringing the demonstration to a close."

I nodded. "Then what?"

"Mr. Weather mixed some highballs, we all had a drink, and I went home. I never allow drinking during a demonstration." After a short pause he added, "Of course I was careful to see that everybody had been properly awakened before I left, and that all suggestions were removed."

"Did anyone go with Mr. Weather when he mixed the drinks?"

"He was kind enough to invite me to see his den—everyone else was familiar with it. He's quite proud of the room."

"Uh-huh. The reason for all these questions, Mr. Borden, is that Jay Weather has had a hallucination every single day since the party. He thinks there's a parrot on his shoulder. I'm pretty damn sure it's a posthypnotic suggestion."

"What's that?" He sounded surprised.

I explained in more detail and he said, "It does sound like the result of hypnosis, but I assure you, Mr. Logan, it can have no connection with the demonstration Saturday night. There was no mention of a parrot or any other visual hallucination. And even if there had been, I'm far too careful and competent a hypnotist to leave any suggestion in a subject's mind after a demonstration." He seemed irritated.

"One last thing, Mr. Borden. Would you briefly describe your demonstration that evening?"

He nodded. "Certainly. I gave the gathering—eight people—a short lecture on fundamentals. That is, some pretrance instruction. Then after a few demonstrations I attempted group hypnosis."

I interrupted, "In other words, you tried to hypnotize all of them at once?" He nodded, and I asked, "What if all eight of them went into trance?"

He smiled. "That would never happen with such a group, Mr. Logan. But I was able to induce deep trance in three of those present, utilizing Andrew Salter's 'feedback' technique in which the subject is asked to describe how he feels and those sensations are fed back to him, so to speak, at the next attempt. Incidentally, I consider that a most important step forward." He squinted at the floor. "Let's see, those three were Mr. and Mrs. Weather and another woman with an odd name. Lovely girl."

"Ayla Veichek?"

"Yes, that's it. At any rate I conditioned those three to instantaneous hypnosis, then awakened them all and demonstrated with only one at a time. That was so the other seven persons present might observe the trance phenomena."

"Just a minute, please, Mr. Borden. What do you mean by instantaneous hypnosis?"

"A common procedure. Once a subject is in deep trance he may be given the suggestion that later he will go instantly to sleep when a certain sign is made or a certain word or phrase is spoken. For example. Subject A is hypnotized. He is then told that he will later go into a deep, sound sleep when I snap my fingers and say, 'Go to sleep.' Then he is awakened, and when I snap my fingers and say 'Go to sleep,' he immediately does so."

I shook my head. "You mean you could go to Mr. or Mrs. Weather, or Ayla Veichek, right now and put them to sleep?"

"Not at all. I told you, Mr. Logan, that before I left the Weathers' I removed all suggestions. Remember, there were five people there who were never at any time hypnotized. Five besides me. Now I'd have to begin all over again, with their consent."

"Uh-huh." I ran over it in my mind, then I said, "Well, thanks for the dope, Mr. Borden. That's about what I wanted." I glanced at my watch. It was sixteen minutes after nine P.M. I looked at Borden again, thinking of the strange power he'd had, for a while, over those three people at the party. I still wondered about Jay's parrot.

I said, "The more I learn of hypnotism the more interesting it gets. Just tell people to go to sleep and, bang, off they go."

He laughed. "It's not as simple as that, Mr. Logan. There are several methods . . ." He paused, frowning slightly. "Well, for example," he said, and left the sentence unfinished.

Then he walked to a corner of the room and pulled a table away from the wall. On it was a large portable record player and another gadget like nothing I'd seen before. It was a cardboard disk about six inches wide, with a black spot in the middle and alternate black and white strips curving from the center to the outer edge of the disk. The strips began almost as pinpoint lines at the center, then widened to about half an inch at the disk's edge.

Borden flipped a switch on the player and said, pointing to the black and white disk, "There are many methods of fixing attention in order to aid the induction of hypnosis—crystal balls, a spot on the wall, a bright object—but

I've found this very effective." He flipped another switch and the disk began to revolve, the lines blending into each other, the spiral almost forcing my eyes to the black center.

"You'll note," Border said in a pleasant, conversational tone, "that there is a definite fascination about that disk as it revolves. I often use this to focus the attention of the subject and to aid in reducing sensory impressions. Then, add some soothing, pleasant music in the background, and the effect is intensified."

He turned a dial and pulsing music swelled from the record player. It was definitely relaxing.

"You can see how this helps," Borden said. "The eyes are centered on the disk and the music provides a soothing counterpoint to my voice. It relaxes you, relaxes you completely."

He was right about that. The spinning disk and the music combined had a definite hypnotic quality even without Borden's voice thrown in. And his voice seemed to add to the soothing, relaxing effect. He was still speaking, and suddenly it seemed to me that his voice changed slightly, became more resonant and took on a deeper, richer tone.

He said, "Your arms are very, very heavy; your legs are very, very heavy," and his voice was powerful and deep.

And I could feel it. I could feel a heaviness in my arms and legs that hadn't been there before. I could—What the hell was going on here? I shook my head rapidly from side to side, got my hands on the arms of the chair and pushed myself to my feet.

"Very damned interesting," I said.

He smiled. "Indeed it is, Mr. Logan. You can see there's much more to hypnosis than merely telling people to go to sleep."

He turned off the switches and the music stopped abruptly. The circle of cardboard slowed and stopped.

I wanted to get the hell out of here. "I'll see you again," I said, and went to the door.

"By all means. I'm quite interested in this parrot you mentioned." He walked to the door with me and as I left he said, "Incidentally, Mr. Logan, I think you'd make an excellent hypnotic subject, yourself. Well, let me know what happens, if you will."

"Sure," I said, and the door closed behind me.

I walked out to the street and climbed into the Buick. On an impulse I looked at my watch. Only twenty-one past nine, and it had been sixteen past when I'd glanced at it before. I laughed at myself, thinking that I was working myself into a fine state of jittery nerves, but still feeling a little relieved that I could account for all the time I'd spent in Borden's apartment.

It was still early. I decided to make one more call, then head for home. I looked at the list Ann had written for me. I hadn't talked to Ann's Arthur, or Jay's lawyer Robert Hannibal, or Miss Stewart. Nor had I seen Peter Sault or Ayla Veichek, who sounded more interesting. Particularly Ayla. Ann Weather had left me in a damned shaky state, and no matter what Ayla looked like, she was a woman.

Then I noticed something about the addresses that made both Peter and Ayla even more interesting. Peter Sault lived at 1458 Marathon Street, Apartment Seven. Ayla Veichek lived at 1458 Marathon Street, Apartment Eight.

I headed for Marathon Street.

There was light inside, slipping under the door of Apartment Seven as I knocked. In a moment I heard footsteps and a tall, thin man in his late twenties with a smudge of paint on his chin and a long paint brush in his hand opened the door.

"Hi," he said cheerfully. "Come on in. Watch your step."

I went inside, watching my step, and avoided tramping on one knee-length boot by stepping on a book next to it. I managed the hazards and stopped in the middle of the room. The place wasn't very tidy, but if he didn't mind, neither did I.

"I'm Peter Sault," he said. "Who're you?"

"Mark Logan, Mr. Sault." I let him look at my license. "I'm a private detective."

He grinned, showing even white teeth. "No kidding? What's up?"

"Just checking on a party you and Ayla Veichek went to last Saturday at Jay Weather's place."

"Oh, yeah." He grinned. "A real ball, that one." Then he sobered and frowned. "Why you checking on that? Something happen?"

"Uh-uh. Nothing very important, anyway. I just wanted to talk to some of the people who were there so I can find out what went on."

A door behind him opened and a tall, black-haired woman stepped into the room. She looked mean. Her hair was pulled tightly away from her forehead and tied in back, flowing down over her shoulders. She had a thin black robe around her and she was as Ann had described her—voluptuous-looking and somewhat delicious. Ann had been right about something else too—I would call her sexy. She had long, long, red fingernails, her mouth was the color of blood, and black eyebrows slanted up from the bridge of her nose like wings, and that wasn't all that slanted up.

She said, "Hello. Party?"

Peter said, "No party, Ayla. Not yet, anyway. This is Mark Logan, a private detective. Wants some dope on the voodoo ball."

She glanced at me, didn't say anything, then walked to an upholstered chair in the corner of the room and plopped down into it, throwing her legs up over one chair arm. She was awfully careless with those long, shapely legs. There didn't appear to be anything under the robe except Ayla.

I told them why I was here and we spent ten minutes batting the party around, with nothing developing that I didn't already know. And they both looked blank when I talked about parrots. They backed up everything Joseph Borden had told me. I was ready to leave when I remembered Ann's telling me about Peter's oils. I casually mentioned "dabbling."

Peter's face brightened. "That right? Well, come on in back—I'm just finishing up a job. Might interest you."

I went back into the studio with him, both of us preceded by Ayla, who preceded beautifully. I was getting pretty sure that she wore nothing at all under the robe. It hugged her waist, clung to the curve of her hips, the firm flesh moving easily under the thin cloth as she walked.

There was a big canvas on an easel in the middle of the room. Beyond it was a low, cloth-draped divan. Ayla walked to the divan and leaned back against it, holding her robe loosely closed. Well, nearly closed. I pulled my eyes away and looked at the canvas.

It was nothing. Nothing to me, anyway. It was colorful as hell and there were curves and mounds and blotches on the canvas, but it fooled me.

Peter looked at me anxiously and said, "Like it?"

I chewed my lip. This was obviously "modern" art. Symphony to a Humbug, maybe. Or Dawn Over a Critic. But I didn't know quite what I was supposed to say without lying.

I said, "Hmmm. Well, indeed."

"Of course there's still a bit to be done before one can really get the message. It's my latest—Diana After the Hunt, I call it. I honestly don't believe I could have got the same effect with any other model. Only Ayla could have provided the essential inspiration, drama, fire . . ."

"Ayla?" I looked at the variegated canvas. "This is Ayla?"

Peter Sault frowned at me. I was a clod.

"Of course," he said brusquely. "It's quite obvious. You see—" he jabbed at the canvas with his brush—"the motif—" He broke off again and turned to the mean-looking gal. "Ayla."

She nodded and shrugged her shoulders, letting go of the robe. It parted in front of her. I had been right; she was wearing nothing else. With apparently complete unconcern she placed her hands at the top of the robe and pulled it back off her shoulders. It could actually have taken only a second or two, but to me the act of disrobing seemed to take a long time, as if every movement was performed with exaggerated, provocative slowness.

The cloth slithered over her shoulders and down her back, baring the bold, high breasts. Ayla seemed almost unaware of her now nearly complete nudity, but her large dark eyes were fixed on me. She held the robe momentarily gathered at her waist, covering only the outer curve of her hips and the outside edge of each thigh; and standing like that with her black brows slanting upward, the full breasts thrusting forward, her legs parted slightly and her skin a startling white contrasting with the black cloth, she looked almost obscenely naked. She made me think for that moment of a hot, lusty woman who would enjoy herself in hell.

The robe dropped to the floor. Ayla turned, stepped to the divan and leaned back over it with her arms stretched above her head. She raised her right leg and pressed it against the cloth beneath her, then lay motionless.

Peter was talking, but I barely heard him. He said something about ". . . chiaroscuro . . . symbolic elements . . . tonal exigency" and many other incomprehensible things, but I was looking at Ayla. As far as I was concerned, she was the only work of art in the room, and she had all the necessary elements, symbolic and otherwise.

Peter didn't remove his attention from the canvas for a moment, but kept on jabbering. With my eyes on Ayla, I made comments of almost wild approval at appropriate intervals, and Ayla turned her head and looked at me, smiling wickedly.

Peter started to turn toward me and I looked at him for a change. He grinned happily. "Thanks," he said. "You can see how it'll be when it's finished."

"Yes, indeed," I said. "I sure can."

Peter turned back to his canvas and started working on it. As far as I could tell, there was no more he could do to it, but he kept dabbing here and there. I stood quite still. There were really no more questions I cared to ask Peter, but I'd thought of one or two I wanted to ask Ayla.

Suddenly Peter cried, "Where in hell is that chrome yellow?"

It startled me. "What?"

"The chrome yellow. That will do it!" He was fumbling through a large box of crumpled paint tubes. "Ayla, where in hell is that chrome yellow?"

She shrugged. Then she propped herself up on one elbow. Her long hair fell down in waves over one white shoulder.

"Damn," Peter said, and he charged out of the room. From out front somewhere came the sound of a door being slammed.

Ayla looked at me.

After a few seconds I said, "Where'd he go?"

"Probably out to the garage. He has paints and things out there."

"Oh. Just to the garage."

She smiled. If that wasn't a wicked smile it would do until the devil himself came along. But it was a beautiful wicked smile.

"Mr. Logan," she said.

"Yes?"

"Come over here."

Her voice was a throbbing contralto. It was deep and soft, like darkness, like blackness; it was like the blackness of her hair and brows and eyes. I walked to the divan.

"Sit down," she said.

I sat near her and she said, "Look at me."

The words surprised me. I'd expected her to say something else. "What?" I said. Unconsciously I had been holding my breath.

"Look at me, Mr. Logan. Just look at me. Do you mind?" She spoke very slowly, almost lazily.

"No. Of course not. I . . ." This was a strange conversation.

She had been leaning on her elbow, but now she lay on her back, put both arms at her sides and extended her legs forward, flat against the divan. She gazed up at my face and said, "I like to be looked at, Mr. Logan. I like for men to look at me." She moistened her lips and smiled slowly. "That's why I pose like this. I enjoy it; it makes me feel good."

She was quiet for a moment, then went on. "Peter looks right through me. But you didn't. I knew you were excited by looking at me. Weren't you? Aren't you?"

"Well, yes. Of course, Ayla."

"It's Mark, isn't it?"

"Yes."

"Look at me, Mark. Sit close to me . . . closer to me, Mark."

I moved closer to her on the divan, stared at her strangely beautiful face, the curved, brazen whiteness of her body. I slid my hand over her waist, caressed the swelling mound of her breast.

She moved her head slowly from side to side, eyes on mine. "No," she said. "Don't touch me. Not yet, Mark."

She took my hand in hers, moved it from her skin, then put her arms back at her side again. Her skin gleamed in the light. As I looked at her, she raised one leg, bending it at the knee, sliding her bare foot slowly up over the cloth of the divan and then down again. She raised it, lowered it once more. I looked at her face and her eyes were closed, but she was smiling.

I touched her thigh, caressed her with an almost involuntary movement, and she opened her eyes. She looked at me, moistened her lips again. "All right," she said. "It's all right now, Mark."

I bent toward her. A door slammed in the front of the apartment.

Ayla's face didn't change expression. I slid off the divan and got to my feet. "I . . . I'd better leave."

"He doesn't mind."

"What?"

"Peter doesn't mind. I'm just a—model to him. Stay here."

I shook my head.

Peter came into the room. He held a silvery tube in his hand and waved it at us. "Chrome yellow," he cried gleefully. I could have socked him on the jaw.

Peter started dabbing blobs of yellow on the canvas. Ayla resumed her original pose. After a minute or two she turned her head and looked at me. Her bright red lips curved softly in a smile. Then she looked away from me again. The long scarlet fingernails scratched gently against the cloth beneath her. As her fingers moved I could hear the whispering sound they made.

Peter dabbed at the canvas. I left.

In a drive-in on Wilshire Boulevard I forced down a hamburger and some black coffee, not feeling very well at all. I spent a few minutes wondering about Ann Weather, and wondering about Ayla Veichek, and beginning to feel even worse; then I drove down Wilshire to the Gordon Apartments where I lived.

I had to wake the clerk at the desk, but finally got my key and took the elevator to the fifth floor. Inside my room, I shut the door behind me and felt for the small table lamp on my right. I found it, switched it on, and nothing happened. The room stayed black and I made a mental note to stock up on light bulbs.

I shrugged and pawed along the wall till I found the main switch. I pressed it and got nothing again—just a little click in the darkness. I stared blankly for a moment, then shock ballooned inside me. Automatically I pulled my head down between my shoulders, remembering the lights had been on downstairs and in the hall right outside my apartment. I had just started to duck, grabbing for my revolver, when the air stirred slightly behind me and my head exploded.

I was floating . . . floating . . . and my head throbbed and protested as if it were being squeezed in a vise. Cobwebs swirled in front of my eyes and I could feel my heart pump and blood slam solidly up into my head. My skull seemed to be expanding and contracting, aching and pounding. I could hear movement somewhere close by and I forced my eyes open.

I couldn't see, and I couldn't think straight. I started to pull myself up, but I couldn't move. Now I could feel something binding me, holding me down. I shook my head, a black world spinning in front of my eyes, and I felt hands on my left arm. I could feel the pressure of the hands on my skin; not on my shirt or coat, but on my skin. I couldn't remember taking my coat off. How long had I been lying here? I tried again to pull myself up, tried to figure what was wrong, what was happening.

Then I felt pain in the bend of my arm. It was a sudden pain that felt as if something sharp, like a needle, had been forced into my flesh. Right at the bend of my arm, at the vein there. Suddenly panic swept over me as I remembered Bruce's tapping his arm at the elbow and explaining . . . The pain in my arm was right where Bruce had said . . . No. I must be out of my mind; that was impossible. But I could feel a strange pressure there now and I strained all my muscles, trying to twist away from whatever this was.

I still couldn't see, but light seemed to flash in my eyes as my head throbbed. A hand was on my chest, pressing me down. Another hand was on my arm. The blackness swelled, grew deeper and deeper. It was as if I were sinking lazily down into warm darkness, sinking and floating at the same time.

It was difficult to breathe. I felt as if I were smothering and I could feel something wadded in my mouth, harsh against my tongue. I relaxed a little. My head didn't seem to be pounding so hard. I was tired, so tired, and relaxed. I could hear a voice now. A pleasant, soothing voice. I was so damned tired.

8

The alarm went off and I propped myself up on one elbow and glared at the clock. Seven a.m.; time to get up. I grabbed the nearer of the two clocks and shut off the alarm, then lay back and waited for the second one to bang away and force me out of bed.

Only this morning the second alarm didn't go off. I finally lifted one heavy eyelid and peered across the room at it. Screwy—the thing had apparently stopped at a little after three in the morning. I must have forgot to wind it, but apparently I'd set the one clock, anyway. My head is always like a block of cement when I first wake up, but today I seemed even dopier than usual.

I yawned and my head throbbed. I blinked stupidly, put up a hand and felt the bandage on the back of my skull. Then I remembered Lucian and that other goon who had sapped me at Jay's yesterday. I had me a score to settle with those boys, and maybe today was the day for it.

The hell with it. I creaked into the kitchen and started coffee, then yawned my way into the bathroom for a shower. In five minutes I was awake and rubbing myself down with a thick towel. I noticed a little red spot at the crook of my left arm. It hurt a little, but it was too small to worry about. I stuck a drop of iodine on it and went into the kitchen, poured coffee and let it cool as I dressed.

I looked into the closet and swore. Where the hell was the gray gabardine I'd worn yesterday? I saw my shoe trees on the floor, but not in the oxfords. I scratched my head and looked around. And there was everything. Clothes folded neatly over a chair, my shining brown shoes on the floor beneath it. I stared at them. I always hang my clothes in the closet unless I'm seeing double or triple.

I tried to think. Had I been on a toot last night? There was that one drink at Jay's, then one with Ann—a strange one, that Ann. Intriguing, though. No more drinks after that. Saw Borden, and then Peter and Ayla. There was a hot dish. That was a wicked smile if I ever saw one. I caught myself leering and straightened my face. I couldn't remember if I'd had anything to drink after I got home. Hell, I couldn't even remember getting undressed. Watch it, Logan, I thought. You must be getting old, boy.

I shrugged and got dressed in brown slacks and a clean shirt, bright argyles and brown shoes. Then I went back into the kitchen for fried eggs. After my second cup of coffee I went into the bedroom, opened the bureau drawer and took out my shoulder harness. I stared at it for a second, and got a funny feeling. No gun.

I looked through all the drawers but the gun wasn't there. That wasn't like me at all. A powerful .357 Magnum is something you don't leave lying around. It took me twenty minutes to search the whole apartment. I even went down to the car and searched it. No soap. Back in the apartment I sprawled on the divan in the dimness of my front room and tried to stop my thoughts from spinning around in my head.

Maybe it was just one of those days. You know, when you wake up and fall out of bed and everything goes wrong all day long. Something was sure screwy. I felt the back of my skull again. My head was throbbing gently with each heartbeat and I wondered if I could have a concussion. I remembered that when I'd come to in Jay's store yesterday, everything had been out of focus for a while. That had been for only a few seconds, though, and everything had seemed all right since then. But it was difficult to think.

I was still sitting on the divan when I heard a knock at the door. It was a loud knock and it startled me. I looked at my watch. Only a couple of minutes after eight. Who the hell would come calling at this hour?

I went to the door and opened it.

I didn't even notice who it was right away. The first thing I saw was the uniformed officer standing behind the guy in the brown suit right in front of me.

"Hello, Mark."

I looked at the plainclothes man. Hill, of all people. Detective Lieutenant Jim Hill, a friend of mine.

"Well, hi," I said. "What's a homicide whiz crawling around here for? Want some tips on technique, Hill?"

He didn't crack a smile. "Mind if we come in, Mark?"

"Hell, no. There's still coffee if you want some." They followed me inside. I headed for the kitchen but Hill said, "No coffee, Mark. This is business." He seemed ill at ease.

"Business?" I asked. "At this hour? What gives?" He bit his lip and looked at me and I stopped kidding around. "What the devil goes on here? You act like I've got a social disease, Hill."

"Yeah. How about coming with us, Mark."

"Where?"

"Downtown."

"What for?"

"It'll be explained."

I stared at him for a few seconds and he stared right back at me. I asked him, "You kidding?"

"No."

He didn't say any more, just waited. I sighed. "Wait 'til I get my coat."

In the bedroom I got the brown tweed out of the closet and put it on. When I turned around, the uniformed officer was in the doorway watching me. I brushed by him and walked out with Hill.

Outside I headed for the convertible but Hill said, "We'll take you down, Mark."

I got into the back of the dark gray radio car with him. It was a quiet ride to City Hall.

We went up to the Temple Street floor and walked under the sign, *Police Department*, then kept going past all the special department offices. I'd walked down here dozens of times, but never with a personal escort. Up ahead at the end of the hall was the office of *Commander, Detective Bureau*, and just around the corner to the left was Room 42: *Homicide*.

When we were almost at the end of the corridor, I said, "Hill, will you for Christ's sake unbutton your lip?"

"Yeah, Mark. In a minute."

We turned left around the corner and went inside Room 42. I'd seen it a hundred times, but now it looked different—the long, scarred, brown pine table at the big windows, another table near the door, straight-backed chairs, a calendar from a mortuary—that didn't help—and the smaller office on my right.

And Grant.

Detective Captain Arthur Grant, captain of Homicide. He stood with his back to the wall, tall and deceptively slim, with a wiry hardness under the ill-fitting dark suit he wore. His shoulders slumped a little, as they always did, and he chewed at his heavy, neatly trimmed mustache as he looked at me from blank dark eyes. Tough, but the best cop I'd ever known, and one of the best men.

He looked tired. There was a glass ashtray on the table in front of him, overflowing with snubbed-out cigarettes, some of them only partly smoked. It looked like he'd been here a long time.

"Hello, Mark," he said. That was all. Usually we kidded around a little, but not this time.

"What's up, Art?"

"Mark," he said, "do this. Tell us what you did last night. You know the routine."

I knew the routine, all right, even without the constitutional admonition. At least twice a week I'd come up here and jaw with Art. I said, "What the hell, Art? What am I supposed to have done?"

"It's important, Mark."

He looked as unhappy as I'd ever seen him. He was my friend, sure, but if he had good reason for whatever the hell this was, he'd carry the ball. I wasn't making it any easier for him.

"Okay, Art. What do you want to know?"

There was another plainclothes man in the room now—a sergeant I'd seen somewhere—plus Hill, Grant, and me. The policeman in uniform had faded away somewhere along the line.

Grant said, "Start with last night about seven. Clear up to here and now."

"Right." I sat down in the chair he indicated and Hill sat across from me on the other side of the table. Art and the sergeant remained standing. I started talking. I told them about my going to Jay's right after seven o'clock—and roughed in for them, briefly, what that was all about. Then I told them about seeing Ann, Borden, Peter, and Ayla.

Then I said, "When I got back to my apartment, I . . ."

I stopped and Hill prodded me. "You what, Mark?"

"Well, I went on in, of course, and I guess I went straight to bed. I must have been tired as hell."

"Must have been? Don't you know?"

I got a little twitch of fright in my throat. Hill was baiting me, but nobody had told me why I was here, and I was getting to the point where I really wanted to know. I said, "Well, I was tired. Frankly, I don't remember too well. I got sapped yesterday, for one thing."

Art said roughly, "What's that? You didn't mention it, Mark."

"That was earlier. Couple of boys were giving Jay Weather a bad time and I told him I'd come over and help out. I didn't do so good. There were two of them and one sapped me while I was playing with the other."

Hill said, "That what the patch is for?"

I fingered the back of my head. "Yeah. Bled a little. Guy must have used a gun butt on me." Nobody said anything, so I finished, "Anyway, I went to bed. Alarm went off at seven and I got up. Had coffee, then you arrived." I nodded at Hill

"That all?" he asked.

"You want some more?"

"When you hit your apartment last night, didn't you mix a drink or anything? You go straight to bed?"

I tried to grin, but it wouldn't work. I said, "To tell you the truth, I don't remember so good. Guess that blow was rougher than I thought. Little concussion, maybe."

Nobody spoke.

I could feel perspiration beading on my forehead. "Listen," I said. "Damn it to hell, what is this? I've been jawing away here for ten minutes."

Art Grant said, "Take it easy, Mark."

Hill lit a cigarette and gave me one. "You didn't go out anywhere after you went to bed?" he asked.

I was lighting the cigarette and the match shook a little. I said, "Hell, I stayed in bed. What do you think I did? Jump through the roof?"

"You do remember going to bed, then?"

"Well, sure . . ." The funny thing was, I didn't remember anything about it. I thought of mentioning the screwy things I'd noticed this morning, but decided against it. I wasn't liking any of this. I went on, "Am I supposed to forget going to bed? Am I supposed to be crazy? I went to bed and slept like a baby. A tired baby. How's that?"

Hill dragged on his cigarette and I watched the tip brighten, then turn gray. He asked, "Not a chance that anybody could have seen you in town after midnight, then?"

"After midnight? I told you I was in bed, Hill. You trying to feed me some junk I was seen after twelve?"

He shook his head. "I was just asking if it were possible."

"Hell, no, it's not possible." I started to burn. Maybe they had a job to do, but I was getting full up to here. "Okay, chums," I said. "What is it? I don't like games and I'm sick of this one." I looked from Grant to Hill and growled, "Tell me what this party's about or I clamp my face shut. I told you all I know, and I've got nothing to hide, as the saying goes. But I'm through as of now."

Nobody said anything for a minute, then Art sighed. "Okay, Mark," he said. "You get it. By the way, did you wear your gun down here?"

That one went all the way in and twisted. I said quietly, "No. Why ask about my gun?" I nodded at Hill. "He knows I didn't bring a gun. I was in my shirt sleeves when he came." I tried to toss it off, but I was remembering I didn't have a gun to wear. My throat got dry all of a sudden. "Spill it," I said.

Art turned and went into the inner office. He came back and slid a gun across the desk to Hill. Then he turned and went into the office again and shut the door behind him.

"Hey," I said, "let me see that thing."

I didn't have to see it again. It was a .357 Magnum with a three-and-a-half-inch barrel. Guns of one make and style are all more or less alike, but when you carry the same gun for years, take good care of it, work on it yourself, you know your own gun.

Hill handed it to me and I turned it over and looked at it carefully. "Where'd you get this?"

"It's yours, isn't it, Mark?"

"Knock it off, you know it's mine. I asked you where you got it?"

"Found it next to Jay Weather's body."

It went right by me. "What do you mean, body?" I asked him. "Jay? I don't get it."

He didn't say anything. I looked at the sergeant. He looked at me. And then I got it.

I stood up slowly and leaned forward across the table, my hands moist against its top. "You bastard," I said. "So that's it. Why, you dumb bastard. I thought you had good sense . . ." I started walking toward the small inner office where Grant had gone. I shoved the door open and Grant looked up.

"Art," I said. "Don't give me this. You find my gun by a dead man, so that means I killed him. You think I murdered somebody?"

He sighed. "Sit down, Mark." He jerked his head and the other two men came in. We started in again. They were as pleasant as they could be, all of them. Nobody bothered me. I had cigarettes, and a glass of water when I asked for it. But we went round and round. I got the story.

A policeman had found the front door of Weather's unlocked and lights burning in the store. He had checked inside and discovered Jay dead on the floor. My gun had been almost out of sight behind a counter near him. Jay hadn't been dead long. He'd probably got it about three or four in the morning.

Finally, I said to Art, "All you've got is that ballistics says my gun did it, and I was at Jay's yesterday. And that I was talking to Bruce Wilson about Jay. I've told you about that damn parrot."

Art nodded. "We got that from Bruce, Mark. It ties in with what you've given us on Jay."

I said, "Art, that's all you've got. Do you think I killed him?"

He shifted uneasily. "Mark—" He glanced at Hill and the sergeant then looked at me. "Maybe I don't. But—"

That was enough. Too much, really. I felt better. "Sorry, Art. Look. Believe me, I didn't kill Jay. If I had, I wouldn't drop my gun right next to him. The only thing you've really got is the gun. I don't—" I'd started to say I didn't know how the hell the gun got there in the first place, but it sounded wrong even if it was true, and I bit it off. I was calm now, and I started thinking a little.

I didn't know what the score was on the gun, but saying so was a weak way to get out in the fresh air. I hadn't said much about the two goons, just that they were bothering Jay and I'd got sapped helping him. And then something clicked. I hadn't mentioned the deal Jay had made with me, transferring me his business, and I had an idea. I hated to lie to Art, but I hated heading for jail even more. I had to find Jay's killer and I couldn't do it in jail.

I said, trying to make it sound convincing, "I think I've got it. All this mumbo jumbo business screwed me up—then you got me mad." I managed a grin. "About the gun: I didn't use it, so somebody else must have. Who, I don't know. But it wouldn't be tough for somebody to swipe my gun."

Art frowned.

I tried to remember if anybody had seen the gun on me last night. I'd been wearing it, but possibly nobody could have told for sure—except Lucian and his chum.

So I tried it out. "I haven't worn the gun for a day or two. I haven't been working. The last time I saw the Magnum was when I locked it in the middle drawer of my office desk."

Art continued to frown.

I went on, "It's the only thing I can think of, Art. It's the only thing that makes any sense. Hill has my gun now, and the last time I saw it was at my office. Somebody must have lifted it." I wiggled my head and tried to look puzzled. "How, I don't know. Or why. Why would anybody steal my gun?"

I left it there. Art Grant looked past me and nodded. I heard one of the men get up, but I didn't look around. I'd shot my bolt.

It took about twenty minutes. In the meantime I tried to frame it a little better by going over part of my last night's activities again, then I carefully went into some detail about the session Jay and I had had with the two tough boys.

"One guy was named Lucian," I finished. "Don't know the other one, but the tough boy was Lucian. I had him dancing, Art. You know, the old two-finger come-along?" I demonstrated with my own fingers, and Art smiled slightly. "Christ," I said, "he must have been boiling. But about then the other one took a swing at me and I lost interest. I'm lucky Lucian didn't crack out my teeth while I was sleeping."

I lit a cigarette and took a drag as the phone rang. Art said into the mouthpiece, "Yeah? Prints? Uh-huh. Let me know. Right." He hung up.

I tried to look unconcerned.

Art rolled ash off his cigarette. I didn't say anything. If this worked, I might get out for a while, but I felt lousy about it; I wouldn't feel right till I knew what had really happened and could tell Grant I'd lied to him, tell him I knew I'd had my gun when I went home last night and that I'd had to lie to keep from being stuck in a cell. He might find out I was lying, anyway, and if he did it was jail for me. Friend or no friend, Art wouldn't go for anything he knew was a lie.

"Well," I said. "What now? Is somebody going to book me? Do I have to call a lawyer and get a writ issued?" I grinned, hoping I looked more cheerful than I felt.

Art nibbled at his mustache. "Don't get excited."

Hill went out and came back with hot coffee in paper cups. We all had coffee. Quite a while later, when I was going over the points of my story again, the phone rang.

Art grabbed it. He listened for about half a minute, then said, "Yeah. Okay, come on up." He looked at me. "Mark, did you know your office was busted into?"

I didn't jump or look stunned. I said casually, feeling like a complete heel, "No kidding? It makes sense, like I said."

He nodded and ground out his cigarette. "The front door was forced and so were three desk drawers, including the middle drawer where you said your gun was. The crime lab boys found a print, Mark. One good print, palm and four fingers, on the top of your desk. Not your prints, and not Weather's."

"You identify it?" I was thinking that from now on I'd polish that beautiful desk every day.

He nodded. "We already have."

"Who?" I asked him. Then, before he could answer, I said, "Wait a minute. Don't tell me a thing. I've got an idea. Have you a picture of this guy?"

He nodded again.

"How about bringing up a dozen mug shots. Any number including this print boy. I'll pick out the one or ones who might hate my guts enough to frame me, because it's sure as hell a frame, Art. If somebody's on my back, it's gotta be somebody I've crossed; this mess doesn't shape up like an accident. Maybe I don't get it, but it looks like it was planned around me."

He thought about it, then took Hill into the next room, leaving the door open. He said something to him that I couldn't hear. Ten minutes later Grant, Hill, the sergeant again, and I were back in the large outside room. I sat at the long table with a stack of pictures in my hand and my heart pounding. "Well, here goes," I said.

I riffled quickly through the stack looking for Lucian's heavy face and long hooked nose—or for his friend—for either of the two boys who, I figured, must have been the ones who busted into my office for that bill of sale. And then I saw Lucian's picture. But I flipped by him quickly to the end of the stack, trying to let nothing show on my face. I didn't find Lucian's friend, but so far so good. Maybe I was in.

And right then I thought of something that almost made me dizzy. It scared the hell out of me. Here I was talking about a murder that Homicide thought I might have committed, but I wasn't in too much trouble, and my prospects were getting better, because all that pointed to me was that my gun was the murder weapon. Except for that, I was in pretty good shape. Jay was my friend; I had nothing to gain by killing him; my gun could easily have been stolen the way I'd set it up; nobody could show I had intent or motive.

That was the big thing. Motive. And Mark Logan, private investigator, had no motive. No motive at all.

Just the little matter of my sleeping with the dead man's wife until the day before he was murdered.

Just that—and a quarter of a million dollars.

9

I was holding my breath. I let it out and tried to appear calm and normal as I looked at the first photo and tossed it aside. Nobody I'd ever seen before. My mind was racing.

Even if Homicide never learned about Gladys and me, if that bill of sale showed up giving proof that Jay had sold me his business just before he was murdered, I'd be it and no argument about it. Even the amount paid was there—one buck. Who'd believe me if I tried to explain the reason for that screwy sale? It would look as if I'd forced Jay to sign over his business to me, then killed him. I tried to swallow, but there was nothing to swallow. My lips felt like leather.

I'd been staring at the second picture for ten or fifteen seconds while my mind raced, but I hadn't really seen it. Now I blinked and focused my eyes on it. I didn't know the guy. I shook my head and tossed the picture aside, then looked across the table at Hill and said, "No soap so far. I better find something, huh?" My voice sounded strained.

The third shot was of a guy named Howie Blore. He'd do for one. I said, "This boy. I dunno, but he might have a grudge. I sent him up for a bit." I looked at Art and Hill. "You both remember that."

Neither said anything.

I put Howie's picture to one side, saying, "Could be. Hard to say what an ex-con like him might pull." I felt a little sick. I mentioned a couple other faces I recognized, saying I knew them but we'd never tangled, then I got to Lucian's picture.

"Hey," I said. "Here's the jerk I got wound up with yesterday. You know, the Lucian I mentioned. He's the boy that learned about come-alongs." Then I shook my head and hoped I wasn't overplaying it. I said, "That's no reason to frame a guy, though. His friend got even on the back of my skull."

I put Lucian's picture with the rest of the pack. When I had gone through all the mug shots, I had a neat stack on my right and Howie Blore all by himself on my left.

I said, "I guess it's no good, huh?"

"He's doing time," Hill said, pointing to Blore's picture.

Art dug into the stack on my right and pulled out Lucian's mug shot. "Is this the guy who was giving Weather trouble?"

"Uh-huh. One of them."

"What was the trouble?"

"Screwy deal. Jay claimed they were trying to make him sell out to them for chicken feed. I told him I'd try to change their minds. I gave you the copy on what happened."

"This is the print boy," Art said. "Those were his prints on your desk."

"Yeah?" My voice cracked like thin lake ice.

It took half an hour more. I could have called a lawyer, but I didn't really need one. I could leave. I couldn't hop a steamer for Pago Pago, but I could leave. In that half-hour I went to the "I" room and dug out the picture of Lucian's friend, one Hal Potter, and learned that Lucian's full name was George Lucian. Both of them had records, but they'd pulled nothing except small time stuff—so far.

In the hall I shook Art's hand and he said, "You don't look so good."

"I don't feel so good."

"Keep in touch. We might pick up Lucian and Potter any time. We'll want you. Might want you before then."

"Sure," I told him, and left.

I wanted to run. I wanted to get the hell out of City Hall. I wanted a drink. But I went straight from there to the office of the police psychiatrist. I had to get to the bottom of this mess, wherever the bottom was, before Lucian and his friend were picked up.

Then suddenly, for the first time, I realized that Jay Weather was actually dead. Up till now I'd been thinking about myself and how I was going to prove I hadn't killed him.

Yesterday I'd talked to the guy; last night I'd had a drink with him, told him his worries would be over today. His worries were over, all right. This wasn't just a halfway funny deal about an invisible parrot any more. It was murder. And even though I knew I hadn't killed Jay, I wasn't clean; and every time I turned around I seemed like a better suspect.

I pushed open the door to Bruce Wilson's office and walked in.

Bruce looked up from a paper he was reading at his desk. He smiled at me and ran a bony hand through his thick brown hair. "Hello. Wondered if you'd be down."

"Do you know what's going on, Bruce? With me, I mean?"

He nodded. "Sure. I told the boys about your talk with me yesterday. They let me know what the score was. It's . . . funny."

"Funny? Bruce, tell me this: you on my side or mixed up?"

He looked at me. "I'm on your side, Mark. So far, anyway. Good enough?"

"Good enough. Bruce, it seems funny as hell to me that Jay started getting hallucinations last Monday, and was murdered this morning. This is Friday—less than four days after his trouble started. I don't like coincidences, and I especially don't like this one."

He said slowly, "I thought of that, too."

"Any ideas?"

"No good ones."

"I suppose you know I spent a lot of time after I left here talking to people who were at a party last Saturday at Jay Weather's. Including a professional hypnotist who was there."

He sat up. "No. All I know is that Weather was killed—and your gun was found by his body."

I went over it all, the party, everything I'd learned. I finished, "And Jay was hypnotized. He was one of the three who were."

He sat quietly, frowning.

I said, "A question. Assuming Jay's parrot was the result of hypnosis, why in God's name would he be saddled with that? What's your answer as a psychiatrist?"

"Well, if it was an accident, that's all there is to it. Poor technique. So you must mean it wasn't an accident."

"Let's assume it was done on purpose. It could be done, couldn't it?"

"Certainly. Well, in that case, there might be several reasons. Practical joke. Revenge for some real or imagined hurt." He frowned and continued slowly, "Of course it would be rather a horrible revenge. Or it could be an attempt to create a neurosis in the man, maybe actually derange him. There might be any number of reasons, Mark. And it could be an accident."

"Yeah." I looked at my watch. It was after ten and I was anxious to get out of here. I still needed information, though. "This guy Joseph Borden, Bruce. Know anything about him?"

"A little. From what I've heard, he seems like a reliable man. Certainly knows what he's doing; has quite a decent psychological background, I believe."

"You know what I'm driving at, don't you?"

"Of course."

"Well?"

"Maybe." He scratched his head. "Doesn't seem to be any connection. Bit fantastic, isn't it?"

"And how."

"Mark, does anybody else know about this hallucination except you? I mean people who weren't told about it by you?"

That didn't mean anything for a second, then it chilled me. "Wait a minute," I said slowly. "You don't think I made up this whole deal, do you?"

"Hold it," he said. "Don't jump across the desk at me. I believe you. But what if you have to *prove* Weather told you all this? See what I mean?"

I saw what he meant, all right. I could have made the whole story up before I killed Jay. That is, if I'd been planning to kill him. Premeditation. I didn't like it a bit, especially since Lucian might be hauled in any minute—or Homicide might get a tip about Gladys and me. I swallowed.

"I'm not sure," I said. "He said I was the first one he told about it." I thought for a minute. "I don't know if there is anyone else. But I'm glad you mentioned it. Well, I'm going after this Borden character but good. Maybe I can find a connection."

Bruce frowned. "Could be . . . but don't assume that Borden's the only answer. Even if hypnosis is the answer, Jay's trouble might date back beyond that Saturday party. Besides, Weather must have been a good subject. Borden doesn't have to be the only man who could have induced trance."

"Swell. That leaves only about a million people."

"There's this, too, Mark. When a man is in deep trance, the control can be passed on to almost anybody else."

"Say that again."

He smiled. "Didn't you read the books I gave you?"

"Not all the way through. Hell, I left them in the office. Meant to finish them last night, but I forgot them."

He leaned back and looped a long leg over the arm of his chair. "Well, I'll sum it up for you. Suppose you had hypnotized me. While I'm in the trance you tell me that Captain Grant will take complete control. Whatever I'd normally do under hypnosis I'd then do for Grant. That's an oversimplification, but not much. For that matter, he in turn could pass control to Sergeant Anderson, he to Lieutenant Hill, and so on. Back to you if you wanted."

I said, "I'll be damned. You're not pulling my leg?"

He looked slightly annoyed. "Oh, for Pete's sake, Mark. No, I'm not pulling your leg."

I asked, "What if I passed control to Grant and he told you to jump out the window? Would you jump?"

"No. At least I don't think I'd jump out the window any more than I'd stick a knife in my assistant. But I'm one of those who definitely believe the hypnotized man can be made to harm himself or others. It would probably take a lot of conditioning and training, though. If Grant, say, merely ordered me with no more preparation than we've discussed, to knife my assistant or jump out the window, I'd probably wake up immediately, snap out of the trance. Might even have convulsions."

"I'll be damned again. What if you were conditioned, like you mentioned?"

"Well, suppose that during a month or two of hypnotic sessions I was told that my assistant was a homicidal maniac who'd sworn to murder me, and I'd have to kill him in self-defense. Further, that he was a mass murderer who'd killed a dozen people, raped some women, molested some children, and so on. You get the idea? It would take an expert hypnotist and a lot of conditioning, but at the right time I might kill him. I'm convinced it's possible, though a number of my colleagues don't agree with me. Probably the controversy won't ever be settled."

"How come?"

He smiled. "Assume that, by hypnosis, I make a subject kill another person. I've proved the theory, but who am I going to brag to? Can I publish the details of my experiment in the *Journal of General Psychology?*" He paused. "But I'm sure it would work. Particularly if I chose a gangster or a hired gunman. There'd be less resistance to overcome. A man who's used to shooting people won't react so violently to the suggestion that he's to shoot one more."

He stopped, and it was quiet for a moment. Then I said, "I think I see. But suppose the guy doesn't like the idea?"

"You forget, Mark. He doesn't know anything about it."

That gave me a little shiver along my spine. "Bruce," I said, "you give me the double-barreled creeps."

"It's just a theory—as far as I'm concerned, anyway. It might actually have been done many times, but I wouldn't know about it."

"Yeah. About Jay Weather, now. I'm going ahead on the supposition that his parrot was a posthypnotic suggestion. Suppose Jay had also been told he'd come to my office yesterday. Would he do it?"

"I don't know why not. If he didn't, he'd probably be a nervous wreck."

"Why nervous?"

"Well, the effect of a posthypnotic suggestion is one hell of a lot more compelling than an idea that just pops into your mind. If it were resisted, then the suggestion would bother the subject until he carried it out. I remember one experiment I did a long time ago—I told a good subject that after he was awakened, he would give me his shirt when I said, 'Fee, fi, fo, fum.' I woke him up then and we talked a while and finally I said, 'Fee, fi, fo, fum.' I purposely chose words that would seem strange and attract his attention to them rather than an ordinary phrase that would have served just as well. Anyway, he got up and started to unbutton his shirt. Then he stopped and grinned at me and sat down. He realized it must have been a posthypnotic suggestion—he'd experienced them before and recognized the peculiar compulsion he had to perform the act. He didn't remember the suggestion being given in the trance, of course, but he recognized the sensation. I admitted that he was right, and asked what he was going to do about it.

"He held out for three hours, got nervous, irritable, smoked almost a pack of cigarettes, finally wouldn't say a word. He was perspiring and he couldn't keep his hands off his shirt. Finally he yanked it off and threw it at me. He calmed down at once after that. I thought that one a particularly interesting example because usually the suggestions lose a little of their compulsion if the subject knows they've been given."

I sat for half a minute without saying anything. Then I got up. "Thanks, Bruce. I can't digest any more now, and I've got some checking to do."

He nodded at me. "Sure. And how about keeping me posted? I'd like to know the score on that parrot."

"Yeah. So would I." I went out.

I sat behind my office desk and smoked a cigarette while I tried to sort out the things that had happened in these last hours. It had been about twenty-four hours since Jay had originally phoned me, and a lot had happened since then.

I looked at the broken drawer of my desk and wondered again about that missing bill of sale. Lucian and his buddy had wanted to buy the business from Jay. Suppose they'd killed him. If they had, what the hell did they expect to gain by it? Of course they knew that Jay had yelled for help. They might have figured that if Jay were dead they'd have better luck with me, or with his heirs, whoever they were—particularly if they framed me for the kill. But how did they get my gun? And how . . .

Heirs.

Wake up, Logan. Go back to fundamentals. When a man is murdered, look around fast for motive; ask yourself who profits by his death. If he's got dough, ask yourself right off the bat who gets fat? I dug into my wallet and fished out the list Ann had scribbled for me last night. The one I wanted now was Robert Hannibal, Jay's lawyer and a friend of the family. His office was in the Sprocket Building on Figueroa. And, I thought curiously, Hannibal had been at that peculiar party, too.

I got ready to go. There was still unopened mail on my desk and I picked up the letter I knew was from Jay. I opened it. Inside was a check for twenty-five hundred dollars. The amount surprised me. Jay had plenty, sure, but I hadn't done anything to earn that much. Not yet. Well, I could start earning it now. Maybe logically nobody owed Jay anything now that he was dead. But I owed him at least this much.

I headed for the Sprocket Building.

Robert Hannibal looked like one of the elephants that another Hannibal had herded across the Alps. Hell, he looked like one of the Alps. Not that he was fat; he was just big. When I entered his cramped office, he was seated behind a small desk that made him look even bigger. He stood up when I came in and he just kept going up. He got up to my six-foot size, then kept going for another four or five inches. He had shoulders to match, and his hands were half again the size of mine.

He smiled, showing me large white teeth like sugar cubes, and said, "Mr. Logan? What can I do for you?"

His secretary had given him my name, but not my business. I shook his big hand and said, "I'm a private detective, Mr. Hannibal. I've got a couple questions you might be able to answer for me."

"Glad to, glad to. Sit right down." He acted overjoyed. His voice was rich and powerful, and I'll bet he cut a pretty figure in front of a jury. Particularly a predominantly female jury.

I sat down and took a cigarette from the wooden box he shoved toward me. He held the lighter for me as I lit it, then transferred it to the cigarette dangling from his wide lips and said, blowing out smoke, "Now we can talk. What is it you want, Mr. Logan?"

I said, "It's about Jay Weather."

He sobered. "Yes. I heard, of course. Terrible thing. I knew the Weathers quite well."

"Have the police been here?"

He nodded. "I imagine they've talked to the family and most of the close friends by now."

"I'll get to the point, Mr. Hannibal. Jay was fairly well off, I know. I wonder if you could tell me who inherits his estate?"

He frowned. "Oh. Isn't it rather soon—"

"I know. I'm sorry if this seems callous."

He inhaled a mouthful of smoke, blew a wavering ring and speared it with the tip of the cigarette. Watching the shreds of smoke swirl, he asked me, "What is your interest in this, Mr. Logan?"

"I knew Jay Weather for years. I liked him. He was a friend of mine."

He frowned. "Mr. Logan, perhaps you're letting your trade influence you unduly."

"He was murdered."

He looked at me. "The police intimated as much. But still I don't feel I should speak of the legacy."

I should have expected that. We chatted some more and for a while I didn't think I'd get any answers at all. But when I finally said I could undoubtedly get the information elsewhere, he started to weaken.

At last he shrugged. "Mr. Logan, I suppose it's largely a matter of habit with me. Privileged communications, you know. It's merely that it seems to me you're placing undue importance on the fact of inheritance. That can't possibly have any bearing on—on Mr. Weather's death." Something seemed to be troubling him. He added, "It's absolutely impossible." Then he sighed and said, "All right, Mr. Logan. Probably you'll read the terms of his will in the newspaper shortly anyway."

I lit another cigarette. It looked as if I were going to have a nice motive laid out for me in the next few minutes, and I was thinking about Gladys and her amorous inclinations. Jay, fifty-eight years old; Gladys, a good thirty and claiming twenty-nine. A lush, bright-lights gal, and a pipe-and-slippers guy. I thought how Gladys had told me she remembered almost nothing about the party—and how Ann had told me Gladys was lying.

Hannibal said, "I suppose you know Mr. Weather married about two years ago?"

I nodded.

"After the marriage, Jay had me draw up his will. I handle all his legal matters, you know. He wasn't as well-to-do then as he is—was—more recently, but the entire estate totaled approximately two hundred and fifty thousand dollars. Roughly, it was left to Mrs. Weather and to his daughter, Ann. In the event of his death, twenty-five thousand dollars was to be Ann's when she reached twenty-one. All the rest went to Mrs. Weather."

I flicked ash off my cigarette into a brass ashtray. That meant about two hundred and twenty-five thousand clams for Gladys, plus whatever Jay had piled up since then.

Hannibal went on. "Then, for reasons of his own, Mr. Weather made a new will about two weeks ago. He left everything to Ann."

"*What?*"

"I should amend that. Ten thousand dollars is bequeathed to Mrs. Weather. Everything else goes to his daughter."

A bunch of questions jammed up in my mind all at once. Why? Why two weeks ago? Did Ann know about it? Why just two weeks before he was murdered? I stubbed out my cigarette and said, "Jay left everything to Ann?"

He nodded.

"Did Mrs. Weather and Ann both know about the new will?"

"Yes," he said. "There wasn't any secret about it. As a matter of fact, both Mrs. Weather and Ann were with him when he came here to give me his instructions."

"That was only two weeks ago?"

"A little before that. Two weeks ago the will was completed and signed. In other words, it superseded the old will from that date. It's the legal document now. Except for the ten thousand dollars I mentioned, Ann is the only heir."

This changed the picture. I began to think the will angle wasn't so important any more. Maybe I'd been too anxious to jump at it. But there were too many other things that didn't make sense yet—the two goons, for example. Jay's parrot. And the transfer of his business to me on the day before he died; and, most important to me right now, the fact that my gun had been used to murder him. And once again, all of a sudden, I remembered the little things out of place, the different things when I'd awakened this morning. I felt uneasiness growing in me. I had to find out more about Jay's death—and Jay's life in the days before he'd been killed.

I lit another cigarette and said, "Thanks. If you don't mind, I'd like to check something else as long as I'm here."

He sat quietly, looking at me.

"The party at Jay's last Saturday. You were a guest, I understand."

"Yes."

"I've already talked to several of the people who were there, so I have a pretty good idea of what went on. The hypnotic demonstration is what I'm particularly interested in. I'd appreciate your telling me about the lecture and demonstration Mr. Borden gave."

"Certainly. I was—wide awake all evening." He grinned. "I'm afraid I didn't cooperate at all with Mr. Borden. Wouldn't care to violate any professional confidences under hypnosis, you know."

I nodded, and he continued. His story was the same one I'd heard before. Jay aped Hitler and mixed drinks at the end of the show, Gladys stood up and sat down when Borden touched his nose. Ayla did a little dance, Hannibal said. Everything was the same, apparently.

I asked him, "Did Borden go with Jay when he mixed the drinks before the party broke up?" Hannibal nodded and I asked, "How long did that take?"

He looked puzzled, but he said, "Three or four minutes. Perhaps a little longer. Whatever time it takes to mix nine drinks. I really didn't pay any attention. Why?"

"What time was that?"

"About midnight then. We sat around and talked for perhaps half an hour, then the party ended. You seem to place strange emphasis on a number of things, Mr. Logan."

"Yeah." I got up. "I won't take any more of your time. Oh, Borden was careful to remove all suggestions, wasn't he?"

"Of course. He did that before anybody left."

"One other thing. Did Jay give you any reason for changing his will, Mr. Hannibal?"

"No. I tried to make him take time to consider such an important step, but it was no use. He was quite calm, but apparently his mind was made up. As a matter of fact, I even discussed it with him again the night of the party."

"Oh? During the demonstration?"

He smiled. "No, that was hardly the time for such a discussion. I went back to his place after I took Miss Stewart home."

"You escorted Miss Stewart to the party, didn't you?"

He nodded.

"Well, thanks again, Mr. Hannibal."

"It's quite all right, Mr. Logan."

I went out of his office and down to my car. Obviously my next move was to talk again with Ann. I hated to talk so soon after Jay's death to those who'd been close to him, but it had to be done.

I wished, though, that my reason for going to see Ann were a different one.

10

After lunch I headed for Jay's house. I started to pull in to the curb, but changed my mind. Another car was in the driveway at the side of the big house, and I didn't want company when I made my call. These were the hours when Gladys and Ann were entitled to privacy, and I didn't feel happy about coming here in the first place. But murder changes a lot of things.

I drove around the block, then parked where I could watch the front of the house. Ten minutes went by; then Robert Hannibal came out carrying a briefcase and walked, looking like a cross between a basketball center and a football tackle, to his car. He backed out of the driveway and drove away from me toward town.

I sat in the Buick for another five minutes trying to make something out of that, and wishing Hannibal weren't the family lawyer so I could make more out of it. Then I drove down and parked in front of the house, walked up to the door and rang the bell.

Gladys answered my ring. She was dressed more soberly than usual, in a dark blue jersey dress. Her eyes were red, and she wore no makeup. She still looked pretty good, but a bit worn.

I said, "Gladys, you know how sorry I am. If you don't want to talk to me right now, just say so."

She sighed and bit her lip. "No, it's all right. Come in, Mark."

She led the way into the living room and slumped onto the divan. I sat down in one of the big chairs. An awkward moment passed while I mumbled again how sorry I was and she dabbed at her eyes with a small handkerchief. Even during the awkwardness and the small, heavy silences, I wondered if she knew it was my gun that had killed her husband. I couldn't have been much more uncomfortable.

Finally I said, "Is Ann here?"

"She's in her room. She's been there ever since the police came early this morning. She hasn't eaten." Her voice was dull and flat. She wasn't the same woman who had sworn at me here last night.

"I'd like to see her, if she's up to it," I said. "Incidentally, Gladys, was it the police who notified you?"

She nodded, wordlessly.

Here I was, talking to the bereaved widow only a few hours after her husband's death. But, probably because of the business I'm in, I couldn't help wondering if two or three hundred thousand dollars would have made Gladys look less bereaved. And it seemed strange to me that she'd take Jay's death so hard. She hadn't been very concerned about him when he was alive.

I asked, "Did the police go into much detail? Do you know how he died?"

"Yes. He was shot. He . . ." She stopped.

"I mean the details. The gun itself."

She frowned slightly. "Well, the police did ask some peculiar questions. About you, Mark. I wasn't sure, I was so shocked and stunned." She frowned still more and her eyes widened slightly. "But now—"

I said quickly, "Gladys, I didn't know a thing about what had happened to Jay until this morning. The police came and talked to me, too. I—My gun was stolen. That's been proved to the satisfaction of the police." There were several seconds of thick silence, and then I said, "I was trying to help Jay. You might say that right now I'm trying to make up for not succeeding very well."

"I see." She looked at me, shaking her head, then her voice became sharper. "I see," she said again. "Dear Mark. Dear ex-love. This must be part of your personal investigation. Isn't it? Is that why? Of course. That's why you went to see Mr. Hannibal." She glared at me.

I got up. "Look—"

She went on, her voice nasty, "Of course it is." She laughed shrilly. "And I thought you came to sympathize with me, to console me now that—Oh, this is unbelievable! Dear, dear Mark. Mr. Hannibal was here only a few minutes ago as Jay's lawyer and as his friend! I suppose you know that, don't you? Were you spying, sneaking around spying on me again? Spying on Ann and me? Asking Mr. Hannibal who gets Jay's money now that he's—Oh! Get out!"

I said doggedly, "May I speak to Ann?"

"No, you may not speak to Ann!" she yelled, spitting out each word. She was on her feet now, her mouth writhing. "Get out!" she screamed. "Get out, get—"

"Shut up, Gladys!" Ann spoke from the doorway behind me, and as I turned she said quietly to me, "You want to see me, Mark?"

Gladys said in a tight voice, "He wants to ask you if you killed your father, Ann. He wants to ask both of us." Her voice wasn't loud, but it cracked like a whip. "It was his gun Jay was shot with, so he—" She twisted the words off suddenly and sank down on the divan. Her head dropped and she sat staring at the floor.

Ann said, "Come on, Mark." She turned and went back into the hall. I followed her. She didn't look around, but went slowly up the stairs to her room on the second floor. She shut the door behind me and sat on the edge of the bed. I stood just inside the door, wishing I'd never come into the house.

She motioned me to a low, damask-covered chair.

I sat down and said to her, "Ann, what Mrs. Weather said about my gun—"

"I knew about that."

"You knew? How—"

"The police. Oh, they didn't say so, but it wasn't difficult to draw the obvious conclusion." She was quiet for a moment, then she added flatly, "It was easy for me; I told you I'm practically a genius, didn't I? Among other things."

She didn't smile. She didn't look very different from the way she had last night, except for her lack of expression. She wore the same knitted green outfit, and she'd put on makeup, probably for something to do. But there wasn't any of her previous vivacity of expression and there wasn't any lilt or life in her voice.

Death affects people in a lot of different ways. Some go all to pieces, others seem to shrivel up within themselves and wither inside first before the pain spreads and seeps to the surface. Others will get drunk. Ann looked like the kind who go on nearly normal for days or weeks, then suddenly come apart all at once. I wondered what she'd been thinking since she learned it was my gun that had killed Jay—if she'd been thinking at all.

She looked at me steadily. "Why did you come here, Mark? I shouldn't think you would, after last night." She paused. "I heard what Gladys was saying. Did you talk to Hannibal?"

I nodded and said, "Listen to me, Ann. Just for the record. I liked, admired, and respected Jay. I wouldn't have hurt him knowingly for the world. But somebody did, and I'm going to find out who it was."

She looked at me, really at me, for the first time. "Did you learn all you wanted from Hannibal? Dad left everything to me. I'm rich now. Gladys doesn't get it, and I'm glad she doesn't. She didn't love him as I loved him." She smiled, but it was all on the outside, just a movement of her lips. "They didn't even sleep in the same room, but I'll bet that didn't deprive her of a good night's sleep. Or anything else."

"What do you mean?"

"You think about it." She looked away from me and added, seconds later, "I know she'd gone shopping all day and never bought a thing. What would you make of that?"

I didn't answer her. That was one question I couldn't answer very well. We sat quietly till I asked her, "Why did Jay change his will, Ann?"

She said quickly, "Why shouldn't he? Gladys married him only for his money. He knew it, so he changed his will."

"Are you guessing?"

"All right, I'm guessing. Dad didn't ever say so, if that's what you mean. He wouldn't have. But anyone would know she married him for his money." Her jaw got hard for a moment and she said, "She won't get it now. She won't." Then she paused and said softly, "Oh, God, how I hate her." Several seconds passed. Then Ann sighed deeply through her open mouth and said, "You'd better go."

"Ann," I said, "I'm sorry. If there's anything—"

"You'd better go. This isn't like last night, Mark. I can't even talk to you today. I can't think, can't feel anything."

Suddenly the wooden appearance of her face melted and she turned and threw herself facedown on the bed. Sobs burst from her mouth, their shrillness muffled by the bedclothes. Her body shook uncontrollably. I walked over to her and put my hand gently on her shoulder.

She twisted around and looked up at me, mascara smudged around her eyes, lipstick smeared redly along the side of her mouth. With her lips pressed tightly together she shook her head and waved past me to the door.

I turned and went out.

I walked down the stairs and to the front door. I didn't see Gladys anywhere and I couldn't hear Ann crying. I heard nothing except my footsteps, and they sounded abnormally loud, as if I were walking alone in a tomb.

I got into my car and sat quietly for a few minutes, just thinking. I'd learned a little, maybe, but whether it was any good, or even true, I didn't know. I still wondered why Jay had been killed so soon after leaving everything to Ann, but I'd convinced myself of one thing: even if Ann did inherit Jay's estate, it was foolish to think she might have killed him.

If I tried hard enough, I might make myself believe a lot of things about that girl, but not that she'd murder her own father.

11

I drove to a neighborhood bar and ordered a rum and soda. While the bartender fixed it I used the phone to call Joseph Borden, but drew a blank. I tried both his office and apartment twice while I finished my drink, but all I got was the buzz of an unanswered phone.

In the next hour I called on Miss Stewart, the woman Hannibal had escorted to Jay's party, and Ann's long-underwear Arthur. I got nothing from them that I didn't already know, and frustration started growing inside me.

Miss Martha Stewart was a plain but pleasant woman in her early thirties. She was slim and well-groomed, with her nails freshly painted, and her hair set in neat waves close to her head. Yes, she'd known Hannibal for a year or so; they'd been to the theater two or three times, and to the party at the Weathers'. Lovely time. Parrot? Why, what are you talking about, Mr. Logan?

I told her good-by and headed for Arthur's. He reminded me of what is sometimes, in school, called a "grind." His chin was fine as far as it went, but it only went about halfway, and he appeared to be fond of biting gently on his lower lip. He was about nineteen or twenty, and he probably got straight A's at school. I didn't even go inside. He looked at me from behind his rimless glasses, nodding occasionally while I talked, answering me courteously and quickly. He thought it was fun talking to a "private eye" and he examined my credentials with great interest when I showed them to him. And, like I said, I got nothing.

This would be my last stop; then I was going back to the office and maybe throw myself out the window. I knocked on the door of Apartment Seven at 1458 Marathon Street. Nothing happened, so I knocked again and a door opened, but not the one I was banging on. Ten feet down the hall the door of Apartment Eight opened and Ayla Veichek looked out.

She looked different. The face was still mean, with pulled-back black hair and slanting eyebrows, but I had taken such a *good* look at Ayla last night that I knew her quite well indeed, and something about her appearance was different. Ah, yes, she had clothes on.

It was just as well. There was more I needed to know about that Saturday-night party at the Weathers', and I was here on business, not pleasure. Almost any business, though, would have been a pleasure with Ayla. She looked good, even dressed. She was wearing a bright print dress of thin cotton—or maybe it wasn't cotton, but it was thin—and she seemed to be wearing it with a good deal of reluctance. It might once have had a V-neck, but on Ayla the V became a U with the obvious result, and the results obvious. It looked as if one good wiggle would dislodge the narrow straps from her shoulders and allow the dress to slide eagerly down to her waist. At least.

She smiled slowly. "Hello, Mark."

"Hello. I was looking for you—"

"Oh?"

"And Peter. Where is he?"

"Out."

"In the garage?"

She was still smiling. "No. Downtown. I thought you might be back today."

"Well, that's not why I'm here. I mean I wanted to ask you some questions. Lots of questions. Both of you."

"Come in."

I went inside and she closed the door after me, then walked to another door standing ajar in the far wall. It led into Peter's apartment. She pushed the door shut, looked at me and shrugged.

"Sit down," she said.

I sat down and Ayla pulled another chair over close to me and relaxed in it, draping her long legs over one of its arms. "Have you found the parrot you were asking us about?" she said.

"Uh-uh. Maybe I won't. Have you heard about Jay Weather?"

"What about Mr. Weather?"

"Somebody killed him."

She swung her legs to the floor. "Killed—you mean he was murdered?"

"Didn't you know about it?"

"No. That's terrible!" She paused, then asked, "How did it happen?"

I gave her as little as I could. "The police found him. He'd been shot. Nobody seems to know who did it, or why."

She shook her head in disbelief. After a few moments she shrugged and threw her legs up over the arm of the chair again. A six-inch strip of white thigh blossomed under the hem of her dress, and suddenly seemed the brightest spot in the room. It was certainly the prettiest.

I cleared my throat and said vaguely, "Did Jay seem normal the night of the party?"

"I guess so. I didn't know him very well. I'd been there only once before, with Peter."

"Peter knew him, then?"

"He'd done some work for him. You know, posters, advertising things. That's how Peter makes his living—commercial art."

"Commercial?"

"Yes. I got the impression last night that you didn't think much of his portrait of me."

I grinned at her. "Hell, I hardly saw it." She chuckled. I said, "You and Peter weren't old friends of Jay's then?"

"No. Mr. Weather liked Peter, so he asked us over, that's all."

"Last night you told me you were hypnotized by Borden at the party. Do you remember anything about that?"

She frowned. "It's not really clear to me, but I can remember fairly well. He told me to do things, and I remembered his telling me—but I went ahead and did them anyway. It was—oh, as if I just didn't care. Borden said I didn't go really deep."

Her thigh gleamed. She swung her foot gently and it seemed as if there were nothing but that gorgeous thigh in the room. I said, "Those suggestions he gave—he removed them all, didn't he, before anybody left?"

"Yes. About twelve-thirty, I think it was. Just as we were all getting ready to go."

I swallowed. "Did you all leave together?"

"No. Peter and I were the first to leave."

"Borden was there when you left?" I swallowed again. My eyes were starting to water.

"No. He was the first to leave—just before Peter and me. All the others, except Borden, were still there when Peter and I left." She was quiet a moment, then said, "Do you like it?"

"Like what?"

"What you're looking at."

By George. I was still looking at it. I blinked and focused my eyes on her face. She was smiling, leaning against the back of the chair, her foot still swinging gently. It was a wicked smile, all right. From all that swinging, the hem of her dress had crept up a little more. And where it was creeping, a little was a lot.

I said, "Well, that about uncovers it, Ayla—covers it, I mean. The questions. For now." I had several other things I wanted to accomplish today, and I was becoming disorganized. I stood up. "So, thanks. I'd better be going."

She got up too, but by sliding forward over the chair arm, the dress riding up her thighs until it was soon doing her no good whatsoever. It was certainly doing me no good whatsoever. It seemed that whether Ayla was in a robe or a dress, that was all she was in. There was still nothing beneath the dress except Ayla and she didn't seem to mind at all that we both now shared that knowledge.

As she stood up, the dress rustled back down her thighs to her knees. "Must you go, Mark?"

"I have to go some time."

"Stay a while longer. You weren't anxious to leave last night."

"I'm not really anxious to leave now."

"Then don't leave, Mark. Stay a little while. With me." She stepped up close to me.

She wasn't smiling or trying to be funny now, and suddenly neither was I. I looked at her black eyes and slanting brows, the lips like blood, the mounds of white flesh caught at the neckline of the thin dress.

She stepped even closer and her arms went around me. I felt the long fingernails dig into my back as my hands brushed the skin of her arms and moved down to her waist. She slid up against my body like a fluid, her lips parted and her head thrown back as I found her mouth with mine and strained her to me.

We clung to each other, our bodies molding together until she pulled her lips from mine. For a moment she looked up into my face, silently, then her hand went behind my head and pulled it down to hers again.

Last night when I had looked at her she had seemed beautiful and cool, relaxed and almost lethargic in her movements. She was different now, close against me, her long body moving hungrily, her lips searching my mouth and her tongue darting and curling. I slid my hands over the swell of her hips, up the arching curve of her back and gripped the fragile straps at her shoulders.

In a moment she moved away from me, dropped her arms to her sides and let me ease the dress from her shoulders and down over her breasts while she looked at me, breathing through her mouth. When I let go of the cloth and pressed my hands against the smoothness of her, she moved her fingers briefly at the side of the dress, then slid it down over her hips, let it fall and stepped from it, naked, toward me.

I picked her up, carried her to the divan and lowered her to it, fumbled with my clothes and then sank to the divan to lie full-length beside her, reaching for her with my lips and my hands and my body. Ayla placed both her palms against my chest and whispered almost inaudibly, "Wait, Mark." For what seemed a long time she held me from her, then she smiled. Her eyes closed. "Hold me. Love me."

When I pulled her close her arms went around me and she pressed the length of her body almost violently against mine. Her lips were moist and clinging as they kissed me and pressed against my flesh and nibbled at my skin, and the long fingernails traced fire down my spine. Then she was softness, an incredible softness, every touch of her hands, her breasts, her thighs, a velvet softness and warmth that swallowed me, enveloped me, for an immeasurable time.

Darkness was gathering when I got back to the Farnsworth Building, went up to the fourth floor and started walking down the dimly lighted hallway to my office. The other offices were dark and deserted now and my footsteps echoed hollowly down the length of the building. I was thinking that I didn't know where I went from here. All my leads were wavering around without purpose, leading nowhere. I still hadn't been able to get in touch with Borden again, and that was something I could work on, but outside of that I wasn't sure what I could do. I didn't have anything definite I could hang onto. As soon as I got the germ of an idea it flickered and vanished like Jay's parrot.

It surprised me when I saw my office door standing ajar, but then I remembered the goons who had broken in. I almost expected them to be waiting inside for me, but the office was empty when I switched on the lights. A good thing, too, because I still didn't have my gun.

It was warm and sticky in the office, and my shirt was clinging to me, so I hung my coat on the rack, then loosened my tie and rolled up my shirt sleeves. As I rolled the cloth over my biceps the dot of red at the bend of my arm caught my eye again. I still couldn't remember where the hell I'd picked that up.

I sat down behind the desk and looked at my watch. A few minutes to seven o'clock. Darkness outside, time to go home and go to bed, and I was ready for bed. I was tired and sleepy and disgusted. I thought about Jay, Ann, Gladys, Hannibal, Ayla and Peter, Arthur, and Martha Stewart, and Joseph Borden. And this whole miserable mess griped me.

Hypnotists! Parrots! The hell with everything. My eye fell on the two books Bruce Wilson had given me, books on hypnosis, and I was griped even at them. I picked them up and hurled them clear across the office. They banged into the door, the door jumped open wider, the books dropped to the floor.

That's it, Logan. Get it off your chest, act like a five-year-old. Well, maybe it was a good thing. It was time I stopped pussyfooting around and shook up a few people. Borden, particularly, if I could only find him. If I didn't like his answers I'd bend him around a little till I got some answers I did like.

I glanced at my watch. Seven on the nose. I might be able to catch Borden at either his office or his apartment by now. I grabbed the phone.

And then I remembered.

I had to go to the Phoenix Hotel. Room 524 at the Phoenix Hotel. I got up, rolled my sleeves down, got my coat off the rack and slipped it on.

Phoenix Hotel, I was thinking. Phoenix, Phoenix—yeah, a big place down Broadway. Have to hurry. It was important. Have to hurry. I switched off the lights, started out the door, started to shut it. Couldn't leave the place yawning wide open. And there were those damn books on the floor.

Haven't got time, Logan. Gotta make it snappy. Phoenix Hotel. The name loomed in my mind. I stopped, looking from the door to the books, and I felt a compelling urgency, almost a clamorous shouting inside me, urging me to get moving, hurry up, hurry up, get wherever I was going.

I shook my head. I was acting like an old maid. I bent over and picked the books off the floor and, in the faint light spilling from the hall behind me, the title of the top book leaped up at me; *Hypnotism*. *Hypnotism*, by G. H. Estabrooks, the brilliant professor of psychology at Colgate University. I'd got a kick out of the imaginary-but-real bear he'd created through self-hypnosis for amusement while he was in the hospital.

I was wasting time. I told myself to put the books on the desk, then get going. But that silly bear stuck in my mind. I had a picture of it frolicking over the beds, rambling through the hospital corridors. If Estabrooks had ever told the nurses that a bear was sitting on his bed, they'd probably have run screaming for a psychiatrist. That brought a chuckle out of me. And then I stopped chuckling fast.

It was too much like Jay's parrot. The parrot Jay could see and feel, but nobody else could see.

A trickle of cold climbed up my spine and touched the hairs on the back of my neck. Jay's parrot. I remembered Jay sitting across the desk from me, his face twisted and old, saying, "Right on the dot, Mark. Every damn noon, right on the dot."

Seven. Seven o'clock, and right on the dot. I put the books on the desk, anxious to get out of here, get on my way. Phrases, pictures, words danced through my mind. Bruce Wilson, relaxed and serious, talking . . . phrases from the books . . . Jay saying, "Felt like I *had* to." Right on the dot, right on the dot.

I didn't know how long I'd been standing there. I peered at my watch. In the darkness of the office I could barely make out the figures. Only two minutes after seven. That didn't seem right. I was sweating now. I could feel the moisture on my face, and my palms were damp. And I was getting scared. All of a sudden I remembered Bruce's saying slowly, ". . . he wouldn't know anything about it."

Wouldn't even remember!

Panic wound itself up in a clammy ball in my stomach. It was crazy. Things like that didn't happen, couldn't happen to me. I stood in front of the desk with my feet spread as if I were ready to fight someone, but I was alone in the room. There was just me and that compulsion in my mind. Then the whole terrible, frightening concept crawled up into my brain.

I tried to compose myself, tried to stand off as if I were looking at myself from another body, and see what was happening to me. I knew one thing for sure: I wanted to go to the Phoenix Hotel. I wanted to go. I had to go. But I couldn't remember ever having been there before. I didn't even know who was waiting for me. And I knew that never in my life had I known such a compulsion to do a thing that I didn't even understand.

Finally I accepted the only answer I could find, the only answer that made any sense at all; this wasn't something *I* wanted to do; it was a thing that *somebody else* wanted me to do. Somebody else's suggestion, in my mind.

I remembered that pinpoint mark on my left arm. Fear leaped up into me. I'm a big guy. I've been shot, and I've had to kill men, and I've been scared. I guess every time I've been in a really tight spot I've been scared, and maybe even more frightened than I was now.

But this was different. It hadn't ever been this kind of fear. This was like having a cold hand on my brain, tugging it one way, then the other, while I followed along without questioning.

But I *was* questioning it now. I knew it wasn't just something I'd brought on myself, I knew there wasn't anything all-powerful or supernatural about it. I didn't have to do anything I didn't want to do; I could resist it, certainly.

I stepped quickly across the room, turned on the office lights. When the darkness vanished, a little of my panic went with it and I made myself sit down behind my desk. I lit a cigarette and dragged deeply on it, filling my lungs with smoke that was oddly reassuring. It was just luck that I hadn't gone out of here without question. If I hadn't talked to Bruce, if he hadn't given me those books . . . but he had.

How, though? How had it happened? Suddenly I yanked off my coat and pulled up my sleeve again. I stared at the little red dot on my arm, my insides watery. When . . . when had I noticed that? This morning. This morning when I got up.

And then it hit me. Hit me harder than anything else had and for a moment I was dizzy, my bowels cold and my hands shaking.

I might have killed Jay Weather.

12

I sat numbly for long seconds staring at the spot on my arm. It didn't seem possible that such a little thing . . . It was fantastic. I didn't believe it; I wouldn't believe it. There was another answer somewhere; there had to be.

But I accepted one thing without further question: that urge in my mind, that compulsion to go to the Phoenix Hotel, was posthypnotic suggestion. It seemed unbelievable, but it was real. And I knew, too, that I was going there. I had to know what was behind this—and who.

Only five minutes had gone by.

Who would be at the Phoenix Hotel? If I waited any longer, whoever it was might get frightened himself—or herself. From what Bruce had told me, it could be anyone, anyone at all. My mind raced back over the names and faces of everyone I'd seen in the last two days, but it was difficult to collect my thoughts. I got up, put on my coat again and left the office. As soon as I started for the Phoenix Hotel I felt better, relieved, and that clinched it for me. I knew for sure.

I stopped in the hall a few feet from the office door. I hadn't thought of it yet, but what if I didn't come back? I went back in, grabbed paper and pen off my desk and scribbled a note as fast as I could write: "Bruce Wilson—Hypnosis. Seven P.M. compulsion go 524 Phoenix Hotel. Found puncture in crook of arm. Might have killed Jay. Mark."

I left the note on the desk and raced downstairs. Outside I jumped into my car, started it fast and ripped away from the curb with the accelerator jammed down. The hotel was about a mile away. I didn't want to waste any more time. And as I drove I tried to think this out. It seemed a little easier to concentrate now that I was on my way, wind whipping in the open window and against my face.

I was still shaken and shocked, but at least I had something to do. I wasn't just sitting, feeling mad at the world and myself, and I felt sure that whoever was waiting for me was Jay's murderer—even if I'd pulled the trigger myself. In a little while we would be face to face. I didn't have a gun, but I had two arms, and my fists, and a lot of good army and barroom-brawl training. And I had my knees and my feet and even my teeth if it came to that, and I'd use any trick in the book against whoever had killed Jay and done this to me.

Sure. And maybe I wouldn't. What if I wasn't able to do anything? I slammed on the brakes and stopped, remembering Bruce's words again, remembering instantaneous hypnosis, the conditioned reflex that operated automatically, making men fall instantly into hypnotic sleep at a word or sign.

What if that had been done to me? I couldn't go ahead like this if I weren't sure. Not if it didn't do me any good to see Jay's murderer and learn, finally, what was behind all this. Not if my brain could be picked clean and then the memory wiped out of my mind.

Suddenly I remembered again all the strange, different things I'd noticed when I'd first got up this morning: the clock, my clothes, my gun. I didn't even know what I'd done on the night just past. How could I go ahead with this now if what I was about to see and hear and say might possibly be erased from my mind as easily as words are erased from a tape recorder? That was how Bruce had described it.

Recorder! I sat for another few seconds with the car motor running, and finally I had an idea that might work and might not, but was sure as hell worth a try.

I started the car forward again more slowly. I could see the neon sign in front of the Phoenix Hotel now, about two blocks away, and then I saw what I wanted: *Dillon's Radio and Television.*

I double-parked outside and ran in tugging at my wallet.

I grabbed the first clerk I saw. "Quick. How much for your best tape recorder? Portable."

"Huh?"

The stupid bastard. "Tape recorder. Quick. I'm in a hurry. There's a bonus in it if you hurry!"

Bonus did it. That or the look that was probably on my face. He said, "The Webster's about a hundred-ninety, plus sales—"

I jammed two hundred-dollar bills and a twenty into his hand and said, "Get it for me. Right now and you keep the change."

He gawked at the money, then jumped about four feet and was gone. He was back in thirty seconds. "Here—"

I broke in "This ready to go? This standard?"

"It's a demonstrator model—the tape's already on. Just plug—"

I was on my way.

In the lobby of the Phoenix Hotel I looked around for a bellboy, house dick, anybody. I was perspiring from every pore and I could almost feel the seconds ticking away. I spotted a young uniformed bellhop with bright red hair and a small red mustache. I walked rapidly toward him carrying the recorder, and I had another hundred-dollar bill wadded up in my right hand. The bill was almost wringing wet.

I stopped in front of him and said softly, "Red. You want to make a hundred bucks?"

His mouth dropped open and I didn't wait for an answer. I said, "There's a party in Room Five-twenty-four. I want inside the adjoining room—either side will do. How fast can you find out if one's empty, and how fast can you let me in?" I gave him the hundred so he could look at it and get the feel of it, shoved my detective's license in front of his face, and added, "All I want to do is listen, Red." I wiggled the tape recorder.

It didn't take him two seconds to make up his mind. He looked once at the desk, then said, "Come on."

We caught an elevator and shot up to the fifth floor. On the way I looked at my watch. It was already seven-fifteen, and I hoped I hadn't wasted too much time. I'd soon know.

We got out on five and I followed the bellhop down the hall. He stopped at 522 and started to knock, then stopped and looked at me. I shook my head. He hesitated a moment, then dug into his pocket. "Passkey," he said softly.

I whispered, "This room empty?"

He shrugged and whispered back, "You got me. I'll let you know in a minute." He opened the door and walked right in. I waited for a woman to scream or a man to start yelling what-the-hell while Red apologized, but nothing happened.

Red stuck his head out and waved me in.

Inside, I looked around, trying to decide where I'd put the recorder. Red pointed at the wall that separated this room from 524 next door, and raised his eyebrows. I nodded, and he walked to the back of that wall and opened a closet door.

"Best place is here," he whispered. "Real thin partition." He was earning his hundred.

I appreciated his help, but I wanted to handle the rest of this alone. I jerked a thumb and he grinned, then went out and closed the door softly behind him.

I found the wall socket, set up the recorder, then took the little microphone into the closet and placed it against the wall. I switched on the machine, putting the switch on "Record," turned the volume up as high as it would go and watched the hour-long tape start to wind through the machine. Then I let out a sigh and left the room. I walked to the door of Room 524 and knocked.

My heart started pounding. In a minute I'd know—and maybe I'd knocked myself out running around with a recorder, for nothing, but I was glad it was done. I felt a little better, but only a little, and then my stomach muscles tightened convulsively when a voice inside said, "Come in."

I opened the door, stepped inside the room.

13

I parked my car and headed for the office and stepped just inside the doors of the Farnsworth Building.

It seemed I'd been a little troubled driving up Spring Street and parking the Buick, and now I let the thoughts crystallize. I'd been headed for the Phoenix Hotel, I knew that. The whole frightening episode of a few minutes ago was clear in my mind. I remembered leaving the office, feeling better, ready to go. But after that it was hazy, unclear.

Christ, had I gone to the Phoenix or hadn't I? I couldn't have, in such a short time. It had been just seven o'clock, seven on the dot, when the urge to leave had hit me. The fright started building up inside me again. I remembered it all, every bit of it; my deductions, the panic, the spot on my left arm, everything up to the time I'd left. The note, too. The note I'd written to Bruce Wilson—unless I was imagining all of it.

I ran up the stairs and down to the office. I flipped the lights on and crossed to the desk. The note was there. I read it twice, remembering. It seemed as if it had happened only minutes ago. I looked at my watch. It was ten minutes to eight!

Then it *had* happened. At least, something had happened. I'd left at five or ten minutes after seven. More than half an hour was gone, unaccounted for, sliced out of my mind. I bit my lips, straining to remember where I'd gone, what I'd done, whom I'd seen. I could even have—killed a man in those obliterated minutes. I thought again of Jay Weather, and a shudder rippled up my back.

I sat down behind the desk and made myself relax a little. I was letting my imagination run away with me. I told myself that I wouldn't murder, not even if I were compelled by hypnosis. Bruce had said that even though he thought such a thing was possible, it would take a lot of time. It wasn't something a man—even an expert hypnotist—could make another do by merely snapping his fingers.

All I had to do was stay calm, not let fear cloud my thoughts, and think logically and clearly. I wasn't some jungle savage bowing in front of a stone idol and believing in magic and miracles. I was an adult, a grown man. I wasn't a machine with buttons marked "Stop" and "Go," not just a collection of conditioned reflexes that another man could play with, not a tool that another could use for his own ends.

But my throat was dry and I knew that right now I couldn't even trust my own thoughts. I just couldn't remember. I took off my coat and jerked up my shirt sleeve again. I looked at the little iodine-stained spot, a tiny puncture scabbed over now. I thought about everything that I could remember, and nothing made sense except that I must actually have gone to the Phoenix. I had no memory of what I'd done there. And I knew I'd probably never find out unless I went back—but I was afraid to go. It was an almost superstitious fear inside me, and I wondered if the truly insane, in moments of lucidity, ever felt as I did now.

It was like living in two worlds at different times, the worlds separated by forgetfulness. It was, in a way, a kind of hypnotically induced schizophrenia, a dividing of the man inside the body into two entities, neither knowing the other. I wondered what the Mark Logan I couldn't remember was like. Probably there were not only two but many men within each man's flesh, a kind of Jekyll-to-Hyde gamut with myriad men in between, all fused into one appearance and consciousness that walks and talks like a man. I was letting this thing get twisted inside me. I couldn't sit here, staring at my arm and thinking crazy thoughts.

On my arm . . . Between the elbow and wrist on the inside of my arm there were two little red dots, not like the other one I'd noticed earlier, but smaller, barely visible.

I peered at them, touched them. There wasn't any pain, though the skin had been punctured. They hadn't been there an hour ago. I was as sure of that as I was of anything.

I sat quietly for the next few minutes, thinking, trying to compose my thoughts and plan. Then I got up, pulled on my coat and left the office.

I stood outside the Phoenix Hotel and looked up at the neon sign. I was scared. If I had been in here once already and didn't remember it, the same thing might happen again. But at least I knew I'd earlier been headed for Room 524; certainly nothing could happen to me in the brightly lit lobby.

I went inside and walked to the desk.

A tall, balding clerk looked up. "Yes?"

"Would you tell me who's in Room Five-twenty-four?"

He frowned slightly. "Well, I don't think—"

I shoved my opened wallet across the desk, the photostat of my license visible. "Look," I said. "It may be nothing, but it may be important. I'm trying to do this as carefully as possible, so that no unnecessary scandal . . ." I let it trail off.

"Scandal?"

"Possibly. It may not be the person I want. If you'll just give me the name?"

He bit his lip. "Well . . . you'll be discreet, now, won't you?"

"Most discreet."

He hesitated a moment, then pawed through some records. "Smith," he said. "J. A. Smith of San Francisco."

"Oh." Smith. I should have known. The "J" probably stood for John. "Mr. or Mrs. Smith?" I asked.

"That's strange. I don't know. The reservation was made by phone."

"Anybody see this Smith?"

"I really couldn't say, sir. We have more than seven hundred rooms here. It's impossible—"

"Yeah. Thanks. I suppose Smith has checked out?"

He consulted the card. "No. Not yet. Not according to my records."

"Thanks very much."

"You'll be—discreet?"

I nodded at him and walked away from the desk. I sat down in a corner of the lobby and lit a cigarette. I was damned if I was going up to 524 by myself. Maybe it was time I called in the police, but what could I tell them? And I admitted to myself I was afraid they'd find out something about me that even I didn't know, something maybe I didn't want to know. I was so confused I wasn't even acting like myself. But I'd rather have faced a man with a .45 automatic than knock on that door upstairs.

There was a little redheaded guy in uniform watching me, a bellboy. He scratched at a thin red mustache and nodded at me. As far as I knew I'd never seen him before, but he acted as if he knew me.

I grinned halfheartedly and nodded. He walked over to me. "Hi," he said. "Everything work out?"

"Huh?"

"I mean upstairs."

"Look," I said. "How long ago was this? This—upstairs business?"

His face got blank. "You kidding?"

"Tell me!"

"Well . . . An hour, maybe less. Don't you remember?"

"No. What happened?"

His eyes narrowed. "You remember giving me the hundred bucks?"

"What hundred?"

He licked his lips. "Well," he said. "I'll—be right back."

I grabbed his arm. "Hold it. If I gave you a hundred, it's yours." I tried to think of something to tell him. "Look, kid, I'm a private detective. Did I tell you that?"

He nodded, staring at me.

"I'm on a job. I—got hit on the head. Just a little while ago a guy sapped me. Look." I turned my head so he could see the patch that was still there.

When I looked back at him his mouth was open and he was nodding his head slowly.

"It jarred hell out of me. I can't remember anything that happened all day. Must have scrambled something."

"Yeah," he said. "Golly."

"Look, kid. You've got to tell me everything I did that you know about. I'll pay you—"

He held up his hand. "Mister, that hundred was the biggest tip I ever got. This is included."

He gave me the whole thing, told me all he knew. It took me upstairs, but not into Room 524.

I said, "I took a recorder up there? Then what?"

"You got me, mister. You chased me out."

"I wish to hell I hadn't, now. Can you get me in that room again?"

"Sure. Come on."

We got out of the elevator on the fifth floor, walked down the hall and stopped next to 524. I kept waiting for somebody to come out and see me, and I was perspiring like a distance runner.

The bellboy got the door of 522 open. The place was empty. We went inside and I shut the door quietly and leaned back against it, breathing heavily.

The bellhop looked at me. "What's the matter, mister?" His voice was loud in the room.

I winced and put a finger to my mouth. He pressed his lips together and nodded, then pointed to the open door of the closet and the tape recorder standing next to it.

It was here, just as the kid had said. I walked over to it. The spool of tape was unwinding slowly, getting near the end of the spool. I got the microphone out of the closet, coiled the wire and put it back into the case, turned the recorder off and closed it. I jerked my head at the bellhop and walked to the door carrying the recorder.

I opened the door and the redhead went outside and looked up and down the hall, then motioned for me to follow him. I stepped through the doorway and walked rapidly to the end of the hall while the kid locked the door.

I waited at the head of the stairs till he joined me, then I said, "One more thing—what's your name, anyway?"

"You called me Red before. Good as any."

I got my wallet out. I'd had a few hundred dollars earlier, now there was only a twenty-dollar bill there. I took out the twenty and held it toward him. "Okay, Red. How about doing one more thing?"

He pushed my hand away. "I don't want no more money. What you want me to do?"

"I want you to go down to Five-twenty-four and knock. If somebody comes to the door, make up something, say it's a mistake or ask him if he called for room service. He or she—it might even be a woman, I don't know. I don't know what the hell is in there. But get a good look. Then come back here and tell me what happens."

"Sure."

"And, Red, keep the twenty." I tucked it into his pocket. "If I had more on me I'd give it to you. You've got no idea, no idea at all, how important this is to me. There's just a chance you'll catch all kind of hell when you knock. Whoever's in there might be suspicious of any interruption. Better if you know that. Okay?"

"Sure thing." He walked back to Room 524.

I went down one step of the stairs and watched, peeking around the corner as I pressed close to the wall. Me, Mark Logan, hiding behind a wall while a kid knocked on a door. And I wasn't a bit ashamed of it. I wasn't going near that door till I'd heard what, if anything, was on this tape.

Red knocked softly and waited, then knocked again, louder. Nothing happened and he banged at the door with his fist. I saw him fish in his pocket for a key. He found it, stuck it in the lock and turned the knob. He looked up at me once and grinned, then went inside.

I waited for about a minute, gritting my teeth, getting more nervous, but then the kid came out, locked the door, and walked up to me.

"Nothing," he said. "Nobody there. No clothes, no people, no nothing. Not even butts in the ashtrays, and the towels haven't been used. Doesn't look like anybody's even been there."

I said, "Somebody's been there. Somebody must have been there."

He just grinned and we stepped into the elevator.

In the lobby I said, "Thanks, Red. And not a peep out of you about this to anyone—don't even tell your mother." I thought for a minute. "And, Red. I'll probably be back. If you can get a line on whoever it is that registered in that room I'll appreciate it. Only for God's sake, watch yourself."

"I'll watch it," he said. As I went out he added, "And thank *you*."

At the office, I reread the note I'd hastily scribbled, stuck it in my pocket, then phoned Bruce Wilson at his home. He answered almost at once.

"Bruce," I said, "this is Mark Logan."

"Hello, Mark. Where you been all day?" His voice sounded funny.

"God knows. Bruce, I've got to see you. Okay if I come out?"

"Sure. What's the trouble?"

"Tell you when I get there. Anything new on Jay Weather since I saw you?"

"No, not that I know of. Not on Weather."

"Anything on Lucian and Potter?"

"No. Uh, Mark, have you seen Borden?"

"Uh-uh. Couldn't get in touch with him. Why?"

"I guess you didn't hear yet, huh?"

"Hear? What do you mean? Hear what?"

"Borden's dead. He was murdered."

14

My mouth dropped open. Borden murdered! No wonder I hadn't been able to get in touch with the hypnotist. Something crawled in my brain.

"Where, Bruce? When?"

"I don't know for sure, Mark. I found out about it just a few minutes ago. Hill phoned and told me because I'd been asking about Borden earlier today. Found him somewhere out of town. Strangled."

I pulled the phone away from my ear and looked at my fingers curled tight around it, the knuckles white and the tendons in my wrist bulging.

I said into the mouthpiece, "How long had he been dead? Narrow it down for me."

"Can't, much. I won't know till we get the coroner's report."

"I see."

"When are you coming out, Mark?"

"Well, right now if it's all right."

"Sure; see you here. I'll put coffee on."

I hung up and looked at my hands. They were shaking.

Bruce opened the door. "Come on in, Mark. Man, you look like you need more than coffee. What's that?"

He was pointing to the tape recorder. "I'll get to it," I said. "Hope you've got time."

"All night if you need it." He turned and I followed him into the living room. There was a big painting of a desert scene on the right wall, and underneath it he'd pulled out two man-sized chairs so they faced each other. Between them was a low, glass-topped table with a silver percolator sitting on a heating unit, two cups on the table, a tray of cigarettes and two ashtrays.

I said, "Really got ready for me, didn't you?"

He laughed. "All but the psychiatric couch. You sounded a little chewed up when you called."

"Guess I am, pretty much."

"Sit down and relax. And let go your death grip on that thing."

I was hanging onto the recorder as though I thought it might grow legs and walk away if I put it down. I carried it to one of the chairs and placed it on the floor, then sat down and stretched my legs. Bruce climbed into the other easy chair and poured coffee. It tasted good. Weariness had spread through me and was tugging at all my muscles. The coffee warmed me inside, relaxed me a little.

"Now," Bruce said. "What's it all about?"

I didn't know how to start. Finally I said, "This gadget I've been hanging onto is a tape recorder. I don't even know what's on it, but something's there. I'll play it for you in a minute, Bruce, but first I want to square a couple things away. And tell you how I got this thing. It—it may be important in regard to Jay Weather's murder." He raised his eyebrows and I added, "Important to my—sanity, even. That sound nuts?"

"No." He grinned. "Not yet, anyway. Drink your coffee and unwind a little."

"Yeah." I gulped the coffee and lit a cigarette while he filled my cup again; then I said, "Bruce, tell me something about instantaneous hypnosis. Is it possible that a man could be hypnotized and then given a suggestion that he'd go back into the trance just when a certain word or phrase was spoken? Or a certain sign made? And, bang, he does?"

"Well . . . yes, of course. But usually the subject would have to be willing."

"Is it possible that it could happen even if he weren't willing? Surprised, say?"

He picked up his coffee and sipped at it before speaking. "Yes, it's possible. As long as the subject weren't actually fighting against hypnosis, certainly. Perhaps he wouldn't know what was going to happen." He drained his cup and filled it again.

The next question was the one that had been digging into my brain. "How about this, Bruce? I've been thinking of something you said this morning—about drug hypnosis. Could a man be drugged, then hypnotized against his will?"

"Well," he answered slowly, "that's rather an odd question. The drug, say Amytal, sort of takes over the will. Once the subject is drugged, the gates are down, you might say, the inhibitions are stripped away. I suppose if you could get a man to let you use the drug on him, you'd be able to hypnotize him once the drug took effect."

"Even if he were fighting against it?"

"But that's what the drug takes care of. The man might fight against the drug, but once it took effect he'd undoubtedly lose his desire to fight."

"Yeah. Something else. This morning you were talking about the possibility of a man's committing a crime under hypnosis. How—Well, let's make it personal. Me, for example." Bruce looked at me sharply, but I went on, "Do you think I could be made to commit a crime under hypnosis? Kill someone?"

He rubbed a hand along his chin. "It's difficult to answer that accurately, Mark. Not having worked with you previously, I wouldn't know whether you're an excellent hypnotic subject or can't be hypnotized at all."

"Assume I'm a good one."

"I still couldn't say. Everything I told you this morning still goes, but you can't pick out one man and say it would work with him. With some, yes; with others, no." He paused. "All right, Mark," he said slowly. "Let's have it. You're on the edge of your seat."

I was. I was sitting forward, tense, almost rigid. I took a deep breath and sighed. "I'll stop jumping around the point. I guess I was just afraid to bring it out in the open. Bruce, I'm afraid maybe I killed Jay."

He sipped at his coffee. He didn't gasp or jump. Then he shook his head. "Look, Mark, get it out of your mind that you might have killed somebody. You've let all this talk of hypnotism and parrots and what happened to Jay get on your nerves. You didn't kill anybody."

"Do you know? Are you positive, Bruce?"

"Well, not positive, of course, but—"

I got up and took off my coat, rolled up my left sleeve and stepped over to his chair. "What do you think that is?" I pointed at the puncture in the bend of my arm. "I noticed it this morning, but it didn't mean anything. Not then."

He sat up straight in his chair and peered at the spot. He looked up at me, then back at my arm again. "How'd you get this?"

"I don't know."

He studied it for a moment, then noticed the two little punctures farther down on my arm. "What are those?"

"I don't know that, either. I got them tonight. Somewhere. Some time. I don't know. I just don't know."

"Sit down, Mark. You'd better tell me everything you know about this."

I did. I started with my getting up in the morning. I told him every detail I could think of. When I got to the point where I'd lied my way out of jail, I skipped the involved explanation of how I'd managed that so I wouldn't have to drag in the whole story of my "buying" Jay's business. I wanted to get on with this, get it out. Bruce didn't move or say anything; just listened quietly and smoked a cigarette. I told him about the urge to go to the Phoenix.

When I got to that point I pulled the note out of my pocket. "I wrote this before I left for the hotel, Bruce. At least I know I went to the hotel, though I don't remember it. Then, the next thing, I was back at the office. Half an hour or more, just gone, vanished."

He glanced at the note and nodded. "Go on."

I brought it up to date. Then I said, "And here's the recorder. I don't even know where the hell I got the thing. Maybe I stole it, I don't know. Am I crazy, or what?"

"You're not crazy, Mark. But God, this is a rotten thing."

I turned to the recorder and set it up ready to go. Now all I had to do was flick a small switch and I could listen to something that had happened to me over an hour ago.

Bruce moved the coffee table out from between the chairs and I placed the recorder on the floor between us. He said, "At least you know what's going on now, Mark."

"Yeah? What the hell is going on?"

"Well, I don't know why it's going on, but it appears that you were drugged, all right, as you've guessed, and in a state of lowered resistance you were hypnotized. And from your description, it appears that it was last night. The puncture in the crook of your arm and the rest of it fit in. Perhaps your conditioning took all night; makes no difference how long it took, though. Once you were in deep trance the entire memory could be eliminated. For some reason you were directed to go to the Phoenix Hotel. Maybe to meet someone. Possibly even to report to somebody. After all, you were investigating Jay's death."

"How about that? I must have been drugged before Jay was killed. Couldn't I—couldn't I have murdered him?"

He shook his head. "Get rid of that idea, Mark. I'd say it's virtually impossible in so short a time as a few hours. Not you, anyway, and not so quickly. Besides, we both know your gun was stolen from your office. I know about that and the fingerprints on your desk. So stop torturing yourself."

"Bruce," I said quietly, "my gun wasn't stolen. I had it when I went home last night."

He reached up and stroked his chin again, his head lowered. He didn't say anything.

"Well, here goes," I said finally. I flicked the switch to "Play," turned the volume up full, and settled back in my chair as the tape began to unwind.

15

Bruce crossed his legs and closed his eyes. He appeared relaxed, but all my nerves and muscles felt taut and stretched, like thin lines of ice traced through my body.

Then I heard soft noises from the recorder's built-in speaker. Just little whispers of sound that meant nothing to me. Silence for a few more seconds, then four or five soft, dull sounds. I looked at Bruce. He opened his eyes and raised his fist and wiggled it back and forth like a man knocking on a door. I nodded.

Then from the speaker: "Come in." It was faint, and I strained to distinguish the words.

There was the small, clicking sound of a door opening, then another voice, "Well, hello . . ."

Now Bruce uncrossed his legs and leaned forward closer to the machine as if to hear better what was coming next. He probably could guess what the next words would be even better than I could. The volume was as loud as it would go, but even so the sounds and the voices were dim and distorted. I knew that the last voice must have been my own.

I leaned forward, myself.

"Mark," Bruce said suddenly.

"Huh?" I looked up. Dimly, from the speaker, I heard the words, "Sleep! Fast asleep. Fast asleep." I said, "What's the matter, Bruce?"

He shook his head, listening. "I'll explain later," he said.

There had been a moment's silence from the recording since the last words, then there was the muffled sound of a door slamming. Words poured softly from the speaker, "Fast asleep, that's fine, you're fast asleep now, in a deep, sound, hypnotic sleep. Going deeper and deeper now, deeper and deeper now, that's it."

I looked at Bruce, the hairs tingling at the nape of my neck. His eyes were on the unwinding tape, but he saw me move and nodded without looking up.

The voice droned on, unrecognizable, speaking slowly, barely audible. Then, "You must do whatever I tell you to do. Do you understand? You can speak normally. Say 'Yes' if you understand."

And then, muffled but distinct enough, I heard the other voice—my voice—answer, "Yes."

This was fantastic, unbelievable even as I listened to it. This was something that had already happened to me, but consciously I was hearing it for the first time. It was terrifying to know that the words that had been spoken, the words and commands yet to be spoken were, all of them, etched deep in some inner recess of my brain, graven there even more indelibly than the molecular patterns on the tape now unwinding before my eyes.

And yet they were all strange to me, unknown, unremembered words and phrases which in an hour I had forgotten more completely than I had forgotten what happened to me on my third day in school or the morning after my tenth birthday. For one whirling, spinning moment I found myself distrusting all of my memories and thoughts and impressions, wondering which were real and which false, even distrusting what I heard and felt now.

I listened unmoving, as I was told by the other voice on the recording to relax in a chair and to roll up my left sleeve. I frowned as the words slipped from the tape. I didn't understand. Bruce was frowning slightly, too, but at the next words the frown smoothed out and he nodded to himself.

"Your left arm is so heavy, so heavy, it is becoming numb and dead. All sensation is leaving your arm. All sensation is leaving your arm. It is becoming completely anesthetized. You can feel no pain in your left arm; you can feel nothing . . ." Over and over again, "Your arm is like an arm of lead and you can feel no pain . . ."

Bruce glanced up and when I looked at him he pointed at my left forearm.

I looked at my arm, the sleeve still rolled up above my elbow. I touched the stained spot at the bend of my arm and looked back at Bruce. He shook his head.

There was no sound from the recorder now but the tape was still unwinding slowly. Bruce looked quickly around, then picked up a burned paper match from an ashtray nearby. He gripped it between his fingers then, wordlessly, he leaned forward and grabbed my left wrist, holding my arm out, palm up. He held the paper match a few inches from my arm, then suddenly jabbed me with it. I flinched involuntarily and he drew back the match and jabbed me with it once more.

I looked at the two smudges the burned-out match had left on my skin. They almost touched the two tiny perforations I'd discovered earlier in my arm. I shivered, imagining a needle being jabbed deeply into my flesh as Bruce had jabbed with that paper match.

Then there were again words from the tape recorder. "Your arm is now completely normal except that you will feel no pain in it. You will remain sound asleep, yet you will be able to speak normally and answer all my questions completely. You will remain comfortable and relaxed, and will enjoy answering all my questions. Do you understand?"

"Yes."

"Why were you released by the police?"

"I invented a story for the police and told them my gun had been stolen from my office. They discovered my office had been broken into, and that the desk drawer in which I said I'd left my gun had been forced. They found George Lucian's fingerprints on my desk top and released me."

Bruce swung his head up and looked at me, but I barely noticed him. My mouth was dry, and I was waiting for the next questions. The volume swelled slightly and faded, the words sometimes becoming almost inaudible.

"Describe your movements after you left the police. Name all the people you talked to. Describe your actions and tell me what you learned."

The words that came next from the recorder were all in my unrecognizable voice, but I knew it was mine. I described everything briefly but in good detail, surprising even myself as I sat with Bruce in his living room and listened, with the wealth of detail I unfolded in the recording.

I spoke in a flat voice with little expression and named each person by his or her full name. I always used the third person and the full name, never saying "he" or "she" and—most disappointing of all—never saying "you" to my interrogator.

I told of leaving City Hall, going to my office, visiting Robert Hannibal, Gladys Weather, Ann Weather, Martha Stewart, Arthur. Finally I got to the point where I'd gone back to Ayla's apartment, and I could feel the blood rising to my face.

It was awful.

I shifted uneasily in my chair as Bruce glanced at me and then away, a slight smile on his lips. In a way it was the most interesting part of the recording, but I didn't enjoy one word of it.

I was growing more relaxed as I listened. My embarrassment was taking my mind away from the more frightening aspects of what had happened to me. And then suddenly I got rigid in my seat. All embarrassment and all ease left me completely.

I was thinking ahead of the recording. I remembered that right after I'd left Ayla I'd gone to my office. Then there'd been the desire to go to the Phoenix Hotel, followed by my recognition of that posthypnotic urge. Everything I'd then done flashed through my mind: the indecision and fear, the note to Bruce, and then the blank that was now unfolding on the recording. But somewhere in that blank I'd somehow got the tape recorder itself.

I didn't understand. If I'd spilled that, why hadn't the machine been found and destroyed? Obviously it hadn't. I looked at Bruce Wilson, wondering, thinking crazy thoughts, unable to pick from my mind which of my memories were real and which unreal. I even wondered for a crazy moment why I'd come here to see Bruce, tried to remember if there'd been any compulsion, any greater-than-ordinary desire. But there hadn't been. It had been entirely logical, the sensible thing to do.

I sat up gripping the arms of the chair, telling myself I was silly, idiotic in my fears. I hung onto the words coming faintly from the speaker, straining to hear what came next.

I was still speaking, telling of leaving Ayla's and going to the office. My voice continued, "At seven o'clock I decided to call Joseph Borden again. If I had to, I was going to beat some answers out of him. I picked up the phone, and then remembered I had to go to the Phoenix Hotel, to Room Five-twenty-four. I got ready to leave."

I was weak, wondering what would come next when the other voice broke in, "That's fine. That's fine. Now listen to me. Listen carefully to me. I am going to give you instructions and you must follow them."

I let out such a huge sigh that Bruce looked up at me, startled. I smiled weakly. Of course. Whoever I'd been talking to obviously wanted to know what I'd done during the day. Inasmuch as I was sitting there talking to him—or her; I couldn't even be positive of the sex because the voices were so muffled and faint, but the voice sounded like a man's—he must have accepted without question the idea that I'd come directly to the hotel. It was the only logical explanation, or I wouldn't have been sitting here now.

I returned all my attention to the recording. The other voice continued, repeating every suggestion slowly two or three times, "You will leave this room and return to your office. You will be normal in every way and continue to act as you normally would. You will suffer no ill effects from this and you will remember nothing from the time you left your office till your return. You will be able to recall none of this." Then he said more loudly, "You will

98

always go into a deep, sound, hypnotic sleep when I tell you to, when I say, 'Fast asleep.' But no one else except me will be able to hypnotize you! Do you understand? Say 'Yes' if you understand this."

"Yes."

"That's fine. Now listen very carefully. You will return to this room tomorrow night at seven o'clock." The suggestion was repeated slowly three times and I answered that I understood. Then, "When I count to three you will open your eyes but remain in the hypnotic sleep. You will open your eyes and in every way appear normal, yet you will remain in the hypnotic sleep until you return to your office. You will return to your office, and you will remember none of this. You will not remember being here, nor will you remember anything that has happened here."

Again he repeated the suggestions, then counted to three. After that there was no other sound for five or ten seconds, then the sound of the door opening and closing. Bruce and I listened intently, but that was all except for soft, whispery sounds and an occasional thud, as if someone were still moving around in the room.

I relaxed, feeling tired from the strain. "Thank God," I said. "I didn't kill Borden, anyway."

Bruce frowned at me. "Kill Borden? You mean—"

"I mean I just didn't know. I couldn't remember anything, and I thought maybe . . ." I stopped as I realized I still couldn't be sure. "At least," I said, "I didn't kill him tonight. My time tonight seems to be pretty well accounted for. Well, there it is, Bruce. The whole damned day. You know as much about it now as I do."

He nodded and lit another cigarette, then said from behind a cloud of smoke, "Some of it's clear now, Mark."

"But it all seems like it happened to somebody else, not me," I said. "It's still all blank, even now."

"No reason why it wouldn't be." He paused, listening.

There'd been another noise from the recorder. I bent over, reversed the tape for a few seconds, then played it forward again. The noise had been the sound of the door opening and closing. "Must have been when he left," I said. "I guess it's a he."

Bruce nodded. "All right, then. We can't be sure, but it's a good guess that you were talking on that recording to Jay Weather's murderer."

I swallowed. "I'd like to buy that, Bruce. It would be an almost foolproof way for the killer to keep tabs on what progress, if any, I was making in my investigation of Jay's death. Lord, I'd report everything I found out to the killer—and I wouldn't even be conscious of doing it. I'd even pass on anything I got from the police." I paused, frowning. "But Bruce, I was just lucky to be out of jail. It's a wonder I wasn't in the can all day." I shook my head. "I still don't know for sure what I did the night Jay was murdered. I could . . ."

Bruce said, "Get the idea out of your head that you killed Jay, Mark. Believe me, it's just no good."

I liked hearing him say the words, but I couldn't help wondering if Bruce actually believed what he was saying, or was merely trying to keep my spirits up.

I thought about it. "But those other things, Bruce. I did them and don't even remember. How do I know what else I did and forgot? How can I know?"

He dragged on his cigarette and leaned forward. "What other things, Mark? Don't let this get you down. Look. The only thing we know you did for sure was to go to the Phoenix Hotel. That isn't such a fantastic thing to do, and even that simple suggestion didn't work perfectly. You recognized it for what it was and managed to do everything you did; the note, getting the recorder, and the rest."

He paused and looked at me for a moment, then went on, "Your hypnotist seems to have bungled things a bit, Mark. If he'd explored your mind more thoroughly, or wiped out a little more of your memories of this day, things might have worked out differently just now."

"You're telling me! I guess that's about the size of what we've learned, huh? I did practically all the talking."

He nodded. "Well, we learned a bit more than that. We know, for instance, that the method used to induce the trance was—and still is, remember—an oral command. We also know that he's fairly careful and that he tested you to make sure you were in trance and he could produce anesthesia of your arm."

"You mean that match business?"

He nodded. "You heard it on the recording. Evidently he stuck something—probably a sterilized needle—into your arm after he'd induced anesthesia. You'd have had a tough time to keep from jumping or yelling unless you were actually hypnotized. He was making sure before he went on."

It gave me a shiver again. "You mean under hypnosis he could tell me my arm was numb or dead, then stick pins in me and I wouldn't jump?"

"You wouldn't even feel it."

I shook my head. "Look, I accept it logically—but I simply don't understand it. It just doesn't seem right."

He shrugged. "Well, perhaps it's not important."

"But it is, Bruce. I'm going back up to the hotel."

He seemed startled. "Tonight?"

"No. Like he said on the recording. Tomorrow night at seven. He'll be there. Maybe I can finally get to the bottom of this. You know I've got to. Otherwise I'm likely to blow my top."

"Yes. Of course. But—"

"Yeah. What if I step inside and, bam, go right off to sleep again?" I shook my head. "Damn it, it's hard to believe. But there ought to be some way to get around that."

"I'll have to think about it. Be simple if I could hypnotize you and give you countersuggestions—but I can't."

"How come?"

"We heard it on the recording. He was smart enough to tell you nobody else could hypnotize you. And nobody else will be able to." He shrugged his shoulders. "Oh, I can try, but there's little point in it. It'll have to be some other way."

I said, "I'm not going to barge in there alone this time, anyway. I'm going to haul along about ninety cops and maybe a cannon. We've got him now—unless he gets scared. But he should still think he's pretty safe." I thought about it for a minute longer. "Here's what I want, Bruce. I want to go back up, but I don't want to be charging around in a trance and never able to remember what the hell went on. If I know what I'm doing—if it's me—maybe I can turn the tables on the son of a bitch."

Bruce got up and began to pace the floor. "It's a good idea, Mark, but there are difficulties." He stopped next to my chair and said, "He tested you for anesthesia this time. If he tested you once, he'll probably do it again. Do you think you could get through that without giving yourself away—assuming you weren't actually hypnotized?" He shook his head. "I don't know, Mark. It would be rough."

"I could try. Maybe I could."

"And maybe not. And if not, you might get yourself killed." He stopped for a moment, then he grinned. He said, "This may make it clearer for you. Anesthesia can be induced with equal success through either hypnosis or self-hypnosis."

"Self-hypnosis? Hypnotizing yourself?"

"Exactly. I developed the ability a long time ago when I worked a lot more with hypnotism than I do nowadays. I suppose you're familiar with the principles. It's the same as the usual hypnosis, only the suggestions are given by the subject himself. Watch this. I'll demonstrate for you, Mark. Then tell me if you think you could manage it without being hypnotized."

He went out of the room and came back with an inch-long needle in his hand. "It's sterilized," he said, and gave it to me. "Wait till I tell you."

Then he sat down, leaned back in his chair and rolled up the sleeve over his right arm. He rested his arm on the chair and closed his eyes for ten or fifteen seconds, certainly no longer, then he opened his eyes and looked at me. "All right, Mark. There's no feeling in my arm now. Stick the needle into it."

"What? Are you kidding?"

"Go ahead, please. I won't feel a thing, believe me."

I swallowed and poised the needle over his arm. For seconds his bare arm was right under my hand, the sharp point of the needle projecting toward it, but I simply couldn't do it.

"Mark," he said, "if you can't even poke me with that needle, how do you expect to sit quietly while somebody else jams one into your arm?"

He had a point. Maybe he really would feel it if I stuck him, and was just doing this to condition me for something or other. "Go ahead," he said. "You don't have to try to chop my arm off. Just stick me."

Finally I said, "Okay, you asked for it." I brought the needle down gently against his skin. Just at that moment he raised his arm suddenly and the needle buried itself into his flesh. It went in at least a quarter of an inch, possibly more, but when I looked at his face it was completely relaxed and he was grinning.

He told me to pull the needle out, and I grabbed it, but it was in so deep that I was afraid to pull any harder than I was doing for fear I'd injure him.

He brushed my hand aside, yanked the needle out with one quick jerk, then plunged it in again, hard. He kept smiling and his face didn't change expression.

Mine did. My back rippled and the insides of my legs at the knees got weak and watery. My stomach churned. Bruce asked, "Do you still think you could stand that in a normal state without showing something on your face or jerking away?"

I shook my head.

"The reason I went through all this," he continued, "was so you'd realize how difficult it is to fool a man into thinking you're hypnotized when you're not. If you really intend to go back to the hotel tomorrow—to see someone who may well be a murderer—you'll have to be on your toes. It'll be damned difficult to get away with, even if you can somehow manage not to be hypnotized. Perhaps it would be better merely to have the man arrested."

"Yeah. And then he clams up. I want to get to the bottom of this, Bruce. Besides, I've got a very healthy personal grudge against the bastard."

"All right. Just so you realize what you're up against. But don't forget, as soon as you walked into the room the hypnotist gave you an oral command to go to sleep. And you did. Incidentally, that's why I spoke to you when the recording started. Just in case such an oral command had been given when you were entering the room."

"You mean the recording? That wouldn't put me to sleep."

"It might. Hypnosis can be induced by records. People have even been hypnotized over the phone when they've been suitably conditioned. Probably the words on the recording wouldn't have affected you, but I distracted you to make sure." He paused, his forehead wrinkled in thought. "That gives me half an idea for tomorrow night, Mark."

"Well, spill it."

"Let me think about it. It's quite a problem. I'll sleep on it. There's a lot of time remaining before seven."

"Yeah." I was wondering if I did have till seven tomorrow night. I was wondering if there were any other suggestions floating around in my brain, suggestions I didn't yet know anything about.

We were both sitting quietly, thinking, when noises started coming from the recorder again. They were sharper and clearer this time. I heard the sound of scraping, as of a key in a lock, then the click of a door opening.

"I remember this part," I told Bruce. "This must be when I went back and picked up the recorder."

From the speaker came Red's clear voice saying loudly, "What's the matter, mister?" Then sounds of footsteps, a grating and banging as I'd picked up the microphone in the closet, and finally complete silence.

"That's it," I said. "All of it. Right after that I left the hotel and called you." I got up. "Well anyway, I feel a lot better, Bruce. Thanks for everything. Guess there's not much else tonight, huh?"

"Guess not. Come down to the office tomorrow, some time in the afternoon. In the meantime I'll try to figure something out."

"Figure hard. I'll leave this damn recording here. Maybe you can get something else out of it."

He nodded, got up and saw me to the door. I went out into the darkness of a warm Southern California night, and I was so cold I was almost shivering.

Back at my apartment, I lay quietly in bed trying to think back over the last two days and pick through my memories and say, "This is real, this happened to me, this I know for sure." It only confused me more. I thought of how little men know about the secrets of the mind, how ignorant we are of what makes us laugh or feel afraid or make love or kill. Year after year men had stripped away more of the mind's defenses, learned more of the secret places and the hidden motives, the results of conditioning, but there was so little we could say we really understood. The mind was still a strange and sometimes frightening place filled with darkness.

I lay awake for a long time before I fell asleep.

16

The two alarms went off almost simultaneously and I was wrenched violently awake. Sunlight streamed in through the open windows. I lay still, letting memory creep back into me as the alarms shrilled, then grew fainter, "pinged" hesitantly a last few times, then stopped completely.

It was eight o'clock. That was right. I remembered setting the alarms last night for eight. I looked at my arms. No more punctures. Everything normal. My clothes were in the closet, not draped over the chair. Everything was just as it should be. I remembered my thoughts and doubts of the night before and shrugged them off. The hell with them.

This was a brand new morning. I'd had a sound sleep and I felt as good as I ever did this early. After a cold shower and breakfast I sat in the kitchen over a cup of black coffee and looked at the day ahead of me.

This is the day, Logan, I thought. Today you get even, maybe. Today you find out what the hell's been going on and fix some bastard's wagon, if you're lucky.

I wanted to get on with it, get moving, do something. I wished it were already seven P.M., even though part of me dreaded that hour, but I was anxious to get it started and over with. My brain seemed clear enough. I remembered everything that had happened yesterday, and some ideas were rumbling around inside me.

I carried another cup of coffee into the living room and set it on the table alongside the couch, then picked up the phone, dialed Homicide and asked for Captain Arthur Grant.

After the usual chitchat I asked him, "You pick up Lucian or Potter yet?"

"Not yet. We will."

That was a funny deal. Where the hell were these two? I said, "Well, brace yourself, Art. I've got a lousy story to tell you. Have you talked to Bruce Wilson this morning?"

"No. What about Wilson?"

"This is about me. Hang onto your seat and your temper. And listen, let me go all through this thing before you bust my ear. Agreed?"

"What the hell you talking about?"

"I'll tell you. Only for God's sake don't send any squad cars out here till I'm finished."

"You nuts or something?"

I interrupted, "Okay, Art?"

"Yeah, yeah, get on with it."

I got on with it. I gave him everything I could remember, and twice while I was speaking strangled sounds came out of the receiver. But I kept going, through the whole story.

"So there it is, Art," I finished. "Bruce has it all. He'll back it up and square away anything I missed. How about tonight? Can you set it up? You know, bug the place, have some of the boys around?"

He didn't say anything.

"Art? Art, you there?"

"Yeah. Damn you."

"And, Art. I'm sorry about that—those prints. That business. I've been—mixed up."

"Yeah, you have been, you bastard. I oughta pull you back in here."

"I suppose I've got it coming. But, listen, Art, how about the deal for tonight? I sure as hell don't want to be in the can."

"I'll talk to Wilson and call you back."

He hung up and I put the French phone back on the hook and got out pen and paper. Then I sprawled on the divan and started jotting down the little disconnected things I'd picked up in the last couple of days. I listed the names of all the people I'd run up against, what I knew about them and their relationships, and I was still playing with that when the phone rang. It was ten-thirty.

Art was calling. "Mark? I talked with Wilson."

"Yeah. You convinced?"

He grunted. "I suppose so. Against my better judgement. You still want to go through with that crazy scheme tonight?"

"You're damn right I do. Any objections?"

"I don't like it a hell of a lot. We could grab this character at the room."

"Not good, Art. What then? Beat him with a hose? I've got another angle. Look. I'll be down later and talk to you about it. Hell, we've worked together before and we've always come out all right."

"Yeah. No screwup like this before."

"How well I know. It's my neck."

"Okay, Mark. Incidentally, we started it already. The place is bugged. The whole deal's almost set. Two plainclothes men are in the hotel now. And nobody has any idea who the hell this J. Smith is. Like a ghost."

"That would fit. Maybe it is a ghost. That's all I need."

He laughed hollowly. "Keep your pants on, Mark. See me down here. When?"

"Say two."

"Right." He hung up.

I sat around the apartment scribbling some more, had lunch, and at one-thirty I called Bruce Wilson. "You got any ideas?" I asked him.

"Yeah, Mark. I think I've got something that'll work. Come down as soon as you can."

"I'm on my way."

By two-fifteen I'd finished listening to Art Grant bawling me out, and we'd at least cleared the air. Everything was set for seven P.M. Detectives would occupy both rooms adjacent to Room 524, with equipment set up so they could hear and record every word and sound. The place would be swarming with plainclothes officers and it didn't seem as if anything very horrible could happen to me when I stepped inside that room—I kept telling myself.

I shook Art's hand when I left and said, "Oh, yeah. One other thing, Art. Tell Hill I take it back—he's not a bastard."

He grinned. "Get on with you," he said.

Bruce Wilson had his feet propped on his desk when I went in. "Hello, Trilby," he said.

"I'm a hell of a Trilby. I've just been singing to Grant, though."

He grinned. "He came in to see me. Damn near exploded, but eventually he calmed down."

I nodded. "Looks like everything's set for tonight. Except me. You're the psychiatrist, Bruce. You said on the phone you had some ideas. Well?"

He pulled his feet off the desk and gestured toward the tape recorder in a corner of the room. "I ran through that again this morning," he said. "Here's how it looks. You want to go back to Room Five-twenty-four tonight, but you don't want to go into a hypnotic trance again at the command, 'Sleep! Fast asleep,' and so forth. Right?"

"Right."

Bruce went on, "Our problem is how to make you resist that suggestion. First of all, you'll be ready for it and determined not to be influenced by it this time. But we have to do better than that, and it's better if you don't hear the suggestion at all! I'll try hypnosis, for negative auditory hallucination, but if that fails the only thing left that I can think of is plug up your ears."

"Plug—you mean so I don't hear anything?"

"That's right." He grinned. "You got a better idea?"

I told him I hadn't and he said, "I imagine when you go inside that room the first thing he'll do will be to say the same words on the recording, the same ones used last night. Possibly he'll point at you, snap his fingers, make some sign. We don't know because we can't tell from the record. But if you can't hear him, and if you look someplace else rather than at him when he speaks, you should be able to avoid any effects."

I thought that over. "Sounds all right, but how the hell will I know what I'm being asked if I can't hear?"

"Might be able to fix that. Maybe plugs that you can take out of your ears. If you get a chance."

I swallowed. "If—Okay. So then I can hear this character. What if he catches on?"

"That's your problem. You've got to convince him."

"Swell." I knocked it around. "That's what I asked for, though. But—what if this character starts carving up my arm, or sticking needles in me? You figure that?"

"Novocain."

I stared at him. "Novocain. Will it work? You can't fill me full of the stuff, can you?"

"Nope. And maybe it won't work. I'll squirt a little into the vein in your arm and hope that takes care of it. I can't deaden both your arms and legs and all the rest of you, but it might help. And you'll just have to hope the guy's careless now, after things went so smoothly last night. If he isn't—well, that's your problem again."

"I'm laughing. And if he sticks a nail in my leg and I jump, then I kick his teeth in, huh?"

"Something like that." He frowned. "Let's just hope he's careless and doesn't pull one of the standard tests like telling you you're going to smell some sweet perfume, then sticking a bottle of ammonia under your nose. You couldn't fake that. Let's hope he uses the same test—if any—that he used yesterday."

107

"Yeah. He should be pretty confident. There's no way he could know we're on to him—at least I hope there isn't."

"There's one difficulty."

"One? There's about a million."

"One big one. You'll remember that when he woke you up before—at the end of the recording—he told you to open your eyes and appear normal. That was right at the end, so it must mean your eyes were closed all the rest of the time. Which means he'll expect your eyes to close when he gives you the order to sleep."

"Yeah, I see."

It was getting complicated. We spent almost an hour going over the recording again and figuring out how I should act in order to appear like a hypnotized person. There was a hell of a lot I didn't know, little things like the way I'd walk and talk and look, and Bruce patiently coached me till he thought I was ready.

What it boiled down to was this: I'd go into the room and as soon as the person inside started to wave his arms or whatever he was going to do and ordered me to go to sleep—assuming things would go as they had before—I was to avert my eyes, then close them and hope it worked. From there on in I was on my own. My arms would be slightly anesthetized, but I hadn't yet figured out how I was going to carry this thing off when I had my eyes shut and couldn't see, and my ears plugged up so I couldn't hear. I was going to be deaf and blind in the hope that I wouldn't be struck dumb.

If all went smoothly, which seemed more doubtful the longer I thought about it, every word that was spoken would be heard and recorded by police officers in the rooms on either side of us—and that was my big play. That was what I was after—words that couldn't be taken back. My words, but also some other words I was after. And that was also why I wanted to do it this way, just the way it was set up. There was a good chance I'd get enough to hang somebody.

And if things got rough, well, at least there'd be cops all over the place. Not much could happen. Of course, I might get myself killed.

Bruce spent over an hour trying unsuccessfully to hypnotize me, varying his technique, without success. Then we sat down at his desk and he said, "That's about it for now, Mark. Nothing else I can do. It's not much, but . . . this was your idea."

"I know. You've helped plenty. One more thing, Bruce. Suppose I get away with this? I mean, fool the guy, manage to get the damn gook out of my ears and so on. What if he catches on all of a sudden and, bang, tells me to go to sleep. Will I?"

"It's hard to say, but I'm afraid you'd go right to sleep. It's not really sleep, you know, but you'd still be under his control."

"That's what I was afraid of. Then I've *got* to fool him. The whole point of this thing is for me to keep my wits about me. If I do, maybe I can cross the guy into some damaging stuff. I want to sew this character up tight."

Bruce nodded. We sat quietly for a while. There really wasn't much else to do. From here till nearly seven there was little to do except think about it.

At six-thirty I used the phone on Bruce's desk and called the Weather home. Gladys answered.

"Hello, Mrs. Weather," I said. "This is Mark Logan."

Her voice got cooler. "What is it?"

"I want to ask you a question or two, if it's all right."

"It's not, but go ahead."

"On Saturday night, a week ago, who was the last person to leave the party?"

"Why, it's hard to say. Either Mr. Hannibal or Arthur."

"Ann's boyfriend?"

"Yes."

"How about Hannibal? Wasn't he with Miss Stewart?"

"Yes. He came back after he took her home."

"Could you tell me what for?"

She hesitated only momentarily, then said, "Jay asked him to. He talked to us for quite a while."

"And Arthur? Did he leave before or after Hannibal?"

"I'm not sure. You know how it is with young people."

"Yeah. Thanks. Is Ann around?"

"Yes. Do you want her?"

"Please."

In a minute or two Ann was speaking. "Yes?"

"This is Mark, Ann. About the party Saturday. After Hannibal came back, who left first? Arthur or Hannibal?"

"Mr. Hannibal? Who says he came back?"

"I—thought he did. Didn't he?"

"I'm sure I don't know. Why?"

"Just wondered. Thanks."

She hung up gently and so did I.

Bruce said, "It's about time we took off. You ready?"

"As ready as I'll ever be," I said. "Let's go."

17

We parked a block away from the Phoenix Hotel, on the opposite side of the street, in a plain black sedan with no official markings. With me were Bruce Wilson and Lieutenant Hill, who sat behind the wheel.

I looked at my watch again. Just a minute or two till seven. It was well after sundown now and the street lights pushed at the darkness. I looked across the street wondering if I'd just get out and go, or if I'd experience again that welling urge inside me, foaming and growing stronger, pushing me to get on with it, get going.

I leaned against the back seat of the car and closed my eyes. It was like being at the bottom of a deep pit, far away from surface sounds. In both my ears were the plugs Bruce had made, feeling as if they'd been jammed in brutally right up to my eardrums. They were a little painful, but they worked. I could hear a shout, but ordinary conversation was inaudible. Bruce had attached a thin, almost invisible wire to the plug in my left ear, the thread running back under the neck of my coat and down to the bottom of my coat where my left hand could grasp it. It was a little like a hearing aid in reverse—sort of a lack-of-hearing aid. I felt as if I were wired for sound, but I couldn't hear a thing.

My left ear ached and throbbed. Back at headquarters I'd tried the gimmick twice, testing it to see if I could yank at the wire and pull the plug out. The first time we'd used a thread and it had broken. The second time, with the wire, the plug scraped out and I thought I'd lost an ear, but the plug slithered down out of sight under my coat.

Bruce tapped me on the shoulder and I opened my eyes. He was looking at me, holding a big, ugly, gleaming hypodermic syringe in his hand.

The skin crawled up my back, but I took off my coat and pulled up my shirt sleeves. It took only a few seconds: the deft plunging of the sharp needle into the vein in my forearm—up high where there'd be little chance it would be noticed later—first one arm and then the other, the dull pain as the Novocain was squeezed from the barrel of the syringe and pressed through the hollow needle into my arm. I watched with a fixed fascination as Bruce's thumb moved slowly downward, forcing the fluid out.

He'd already warned me that there was such a network of veins in the arm that this was just a gamble, that chances were it wouldn't numb enough of my arm to guarantee anything. Even so, I felt better. I wanted all I could get in my favor. Then he was finished and shook his head, saying something I couldn't distinguish, and clapped me gently on the back before he put the hypodermic kit into his little black case. I leaned back and closed my eyes again, my arms tingling slightly. I waited.

Then it came.

Just the breath of a thought: let's go, Logan. Let's get going, get to the Phoenix. I tested the impulse, waited, that slight, dim fear of the strangeness starting through me again. I waited till I was sure, while the force of the urge grew stronger and more demanding even though I knew what was happening and why it was happening, and the fear grew a little stronger, too. I sat quietly for another few minutes before I nodded to Bruce and Hill and got out of the car.

I slammed the car door behind me, then turned to see if it had actually closed. I hadn't heard it. I looked carefully up and down the street, watching for the cars I couldn't hear. The blaring of a car horn penetrated my consciousness dimly, and I waited for a moment before starting across the street.

They planned to follow me later. I didn't want anything to spoil the play now. I'd had plenty of time to think, and sitting in the car with the sound blotted from my mind I'd once again gone over all the little things I'd put together for an answer.

There had been no report yet, but I thought I knew who would be up there in the room ahead of me. It didn't make any difference whether or not I had it all figured out before the showdown. We'd be face to face in another minute. But there was one way every odd part of this seemed to fit together and make sense.

Inside the big lobby I looked around and then walked to the elevator, moving in a great pool of silence. A few feet ahead of me an extremely fat man was arguing with another man. The fat man's cheeks wiggled and his fleshy lips twisted violently, but no sound reached me.

I felt almost disembodied, floating, and I could see other people talking now; the clerk at the desk, a laughing young woman with her mouth stretched wide. I couldn't help thinking how strange and different the world would be if everyone were totally deaf: faces without animation, no shouting, distorted faces with snarling lips and staring eyes. And how carefully every word would be weighed before it was spelled out on hands or paper, or even in books; no whispered words of endearment caressing the darkness of a room; no music, no sound of wind or rain. How strange and silent a world this must be for the deaf. I had never thought of it before.

I grinned wryly to myself. Hell of a thing to be thinking about now. I poked the elevator button and shook my head. Get with it, Logan. Look alive. Won't be long now. Start thinking about what's up there.

The elevator stopped and the door opened soundlessly. Nobody else got in and we started up. The elevator girl looked at me and her mouth moved, blah, blah, blah. I could almost distinguish the words by watching her lips, but the sound was only a slight pressure against my ears.

I said, "Five," hearing the word rumble inside my head.

At my floor I stepped into the hall and waited till the elevator started down, then walked to the door of Room 524 and stopped. At the end of the hall, another forty feet beyond me, a man in a dark blue suit rested his foot on a tall, sand-filled cigarette receptacle, fumbling with the lace on his shoe.

I knocked.

Nothing happened. Nothing at all.

I got a tight, strained feeling in my chest. My heart pounded louder, blood drumming liquidly against my ears. When I'd knocked, my arm had felt slightly numb, moving clumsily. I'd have to watch that. My fingers felt stiff and unmanageable, like the wooden digits of a puppet.

I started to knock again—then swore silently to myself. The last time I'd been told to come in. I'd been waiting for the door to open, but naturally I wouldn't have heard a voice from inside. One mistake so far. I couldn't afford any more. I grabbed the doorknob, twisted it and stepped into the room.

There he was, towering over me. "Hello, Mr. Hannibal," I said, trying to make my voice sound surprised.

He was smiling pleasantly, his large white teeth gleaming. I thought again of even, rectangular sugar cubes. He had inhaled a cigarette and smoke drifted lazily out of his mouth as he raised his right arm, the smile still on his face, and pointed a long index at me.

Now! Now, Logan! This was the moment all the planning had been for. Don't mess it up.

For a moment I was frozen in a kind of fascination, then I forced my eyes up toward the ceiling, not looking at the lawyer, clearing my throat while I pushed words, thoughts, anything through my mind. Words, titles of books, obscenities, *anything, anything, Ann, Ayla, Jay, bastardly bastard, kill you and cut out your heart Mary had a little lamb* . . .

I closed my eyes, tilted my head back slightly, forced my features to relax, and barely cracked my eyelids. I had to see him, had to see what he was doing and try to figure out what he was saying to me. I couldn't hear him and this was the worst spot; if I got over this I might be all right.

Was I over it? How was I supposed to feel? I felt all right, felt normal. I could see Hannibal dimly, blurred, as if there were a film between us. I was afraid to open my eyes wider for fear he'd become suspicious—if he wasn't already. I saw his hand move; he was stepping toward me now, his lips moving. Then he gripped my arm gently and led me toward a deep chair. I walked to it, saw his lips move, felt the slight pressure against my eardrums. I sat down, holding my breath.

Hannibal turned and walked away from me toward the door. His back was turned and I yanked at the fine wire attached to the plug in my ear, yanked again with no result. I reached up in desperation and dug at the plugs in both ears, watching Hannibal and hoping he wouldn't turn and look at me, ripping with my fingernails, and pain swelled in my head as suddenly I could hear again.

The door slammed and I dropped the little plugs into the seat and tried to hide the wire thread, watching Hannibal from the corner of my eye as he turned a key in the lock. Then I forced my hands to lie still in my lap, my head resting on the cushion of the chair behind me as Hannibal turned and walked back in front of me. My eyes were slitted and I could dimly see him pull up a straight-backed chair close to me and sit down in it, crossing his long legs.

He leaned forward and began to speak softly in his deep, rich voice. "You are sound asleep, sound asleep, going deeper and deeper into a pleasant, comfortable sleep, a deep, sound, hypnotic sleep."

He spoke very slowly, his words whispering against my ears. I tried not to listen, kept telling myself, you're okay, Logan. You're in. This guy's a jerk. Be Happy, Go Lucky. I forced my mind away from his words, tried to fill my mind with other thoughts, a part of my mind registering the words he was saying.

"Sound asleep, going deeper and deeper now . . ."

Hallelujah I'm a bum again you are my sunshine you are my sunshine clap clap clap clap vo do de oh do . . .

". . . everything that I tell you to do. Do you understand? Say 'Yes' if you understand."

"Yes." *Yes we have no bananas we have no bananas* . . .

". . . no pain in your right arm . . ."

Ain't no pain, Novocain, Vivian Blaine, Old MacDonald had a farm, eeyi eeyi . . .

Hannibal had a long needle in his right hand now. Apparently he wasn't being as careless as I'd hoped.

"Roll up your sleeve."

My coat was still on. I pulled the sleeve up, unbuttoned my shirt and pulled it halfway up my arm. Hannibal grabbed my wrist in his big hand and placed my arm on the arm of the chair. I could feel his fingers tight on my wrist.

Christ, I wasn't going to like this. I knew I was all right now, in complete possession of my faculties, my sight, hearing, mind, everything. But I wondered what would happen if I jumped. What would happen if he were startled and suddenly looked at me—now that I could hear—and said, "Sleep! Fast asleep!"

I forced myself to relax, concentrated on a stained spot on the carpet. I thought of the needle buried in Bruce's arm last night, forced my mind away from it, strained to make my mind blank. I felt the needle, felt it as it went in, but it was like the touch of a thick finger, though there was pain, and I made myself hold still. Then I felt the touch again, sharper pain this time.

Hannibal leaned back, looking pleased. I watched him from the tiny space under my lids as he started talking to me. He was satisfied. I was pretty well satisfied, myself. If I played it smart now, I'd have the bastard where I wanted him.

He said, "You will remain sound asleep and listen only to my voice. You will be able to speak normally and answer all my questions. Do you understand?"

"Yes." *You're gonna get a surprise, you bastard.*

"Describe your movements and activities today. Tell me everything you did. Tell me the people you talked to and what you have learned."

He repeated it all, then sat back and waited for me.

I started in, speaking in a dull, flat voice, keeping my face immobile. I told him of getting up in the morning, and I lied like a trooper while he drank it all in. Suddenly I started enjoying this, feeling a kind of power over Hannibal replacing the power he'd had over me, and I was seized with an insane desire to laugh.

I fought against it, keeping my voice expressionless, but it was like suddenly remembering the tag line to a funny story during a solemn service in church. I fought down the impulse and continued talking.

Finally I said, "This afternoon I thought a lot about all the people in the case, and the funny angles, and who would gain what when Jay was dead. I thought a lot about Jay's two wills—and about the most recent one leaving everything to Ann. It looked bad for Ann then, but I knew Jay must have had good reason to change his will—probably when he finally realized Gladys was only after his money and when he was sure she was cheating on him. He must have at least suspected her of cheating, because even Ann seemed to know it. Gladys was only half Jay's age and she was playing around plenty. Probably with several people . . . including you."

Hannibal wasn't smiling now. His long face was stony and he licked his lips. He lit a cigarette while I watched him with my eyelids quivering a little. I kept it going, speaking in the dull, flat voice.

"But Ann got farther in the clear when I realized that a man who saw invisible parrots might well be judged insane. And such proof of insanity would be enough to have the later will declared invalid. Gladys started looking very important to me then—and so did Jay's parrot. Gladys got even more important when I remembered that Jay had told me if anything happened to him I was to see to it that Ann got his business. Ann, not Gladys. And then I realized that a lawyer—especially Jay's lawyer—should know all these things. It started making sense."

Hannibal suddenly got up, and my throat muscles constricted as I tried to think where I'd slipped up in my story. But he merely turned and opened a suitcase on the floor behind him. He ignored me, as if I were only a piece of furniture, reached inside the suitcase, and I saw the bright flash of light on a hypodermic syringe. It was like the one Bruce had used on me earlier this evening, but Hannibal was filling the syringe with fluid from a small vial capped with brown rubber, and I had an idea it wasn't Novocain.

Then all at once I realized this was something he must have planned all along, and one part of my mind kept me talking steadily while with another part I tried to figure out what he was up to. Until this moment I probably hadn't seemed dangerous to him. Now I was. And he obviously felt sure he was getting the truth from me, so it wouldn't be Amytal or any other of the so-called truth serums. I didn't like the other idea scuttling through my brain.

I kept pushing the words out. "When it all fit," I said, "I realized that the party at Jay's last Saturday night was the turning point, though the motive went back farther. Murder for a fat inheritance is common enough, and the party was given right after Jay had drawn up his second will. Murder may not have been planned till later, but that party was what started the ball rolling. The important things were Jay's money and business. If they could be gotten without killing Jay, all the better. Enter hypnotism. It looked as if Borden did the hypnotizing at the party, then got Jay alone—mixing drinks about midnight as the result of a posthypnotic suggestion Borden gave him earlier—and then told Jay that hypnotic control was transferred to you or to Gladys. It wasn't till about half an hour later, when everybody was ready to leave, that Borden removed all suggestions—and by that time Jay was under your control."

Hannibal had come back and was seated in the chair again, the hypodermic almost lost in his big hand, the long, thin needle projecting out toward me. His face was hard and his mouth was twisted a little as he looked at me.

I went on, "You took Miss Stewart home, then returned to the Weathers'. You couldn't be sure that someone might not have seen you return to the house so you played it smart. You didn't even try to keep it secret that you'd returned. You could always explain that Jay had asked you to come back—and he was already under your hypnotic control. Now you had plenty of time to work on Jay, and give him all the suggestions and posthypnotic suggestions you wanted to, and you saddled Jay with the parrot that was to plant the insanity angle, or maybe actually force him into a sanitarium."

I was having trouble keeping my voice flat and expressionless, and maybe I was going too far with my spiel, but Hannibal still seemed secure in the belief that I was giving him exactly what I thought was true. He held the hypodermic in front of his eyes and gently squeezed the plunger. A little drop of colorless fluid oozed from the slanted, hollow point of the needle.

I said, "Then trouble started. Besides saddling Jay with the parrot, you'd given him the suggestion that he'd sell out. You sent a couple of goons named Lucian and Potter around to buy the business from him for next to nothing. They'd probably have got it for you in time—except that Jay sold it to me. Jay must already have been leery of Gladys and you—I realized that much when I remembered he had consulted Cohen and Fisk about the sale instead of you, his regular lawyer—and, too, it seemed to me he must have been suspicious of Gladys because he didn't want to tell her anything about his hallucinations.

"And there were a few other things that seemed screwy to me. Jay gave me a check that was far too big for the little I was apparently to do for him, and it seemed strange that two goons would single out Weather's, of all the spots in L.A., for a strong-arm play.

"Anyway, when your two musclemen stole the bill of sale from me and took it to you and Gladys, you must have felt that I was really getting in your hair, messing up the deal, getting dangerous. And right then I popped in on Gladys and started asking questions about Jay and hypnosis. She hadn't expected any investigation, certainly not so soon, and, off guard, she tried to cover up by saying that she remembered nothing about the party. She must have phoned you right after I left her to talk with the party guests, and that's where the violence started—kill Jay; make Mark Logan the patsy. It must have looked beautiful. With Jay dead the last will would appear valid and apparently Ann would inherit, so even if I squirmed out from under, suspicion would probably progress to Ann. If Ann should happen to pull a rap, then the wife, as the other heir, would collect Ann's share. Even if Ann were cleared and the hubbub died down, you still had the insanity angle to pull. Neat."

Hannibal didn't look at me, just listened, his eyes fixed on the hypodermic in his hand. I said, "So, with Jay already giving you a fish eye, and with visions of more than a quarter of a million dollars flying away, you started in. Later that night, Thursday, you got into my apartment and waited for me, drugged me, hypnotized me, worked on me and gave me the suggestion that I'd remember none of it. Then, with my gun, you killed Jay.

"It must have looked to you as if you were killing two birds with one stone—you'd get rid of Jay, setting up the inheritance play, and you'd get rid of me at the same time. I wouldn't have an alibi, and my gun was used as the murder weapon. If I got stuck in jail, fine—you'd be clean. But if I got out some way you'd want to know why, and you'd want to know everything I knew, especially what I'd learned from the cops themselves. That was simple, too. Another posthypnotic suggestion for me to visit you here at this hotel. Pick my brain; get rid of me if I got too close, too dangerous."

Now I was really going too far. In another moment I'd have him wondering and the element of surprise would be lost. This seemed as good a time as any, so I finished it off.

I said, still in the same flat voice of the hypnotized man I was pretending to be, "That was all I'd managed to figure out when I had to come here. But it's all about the way it happened, isn't it, Hannibal?"

He wasn't looking at me. He was still staring fixedly at the hypodermic, and I opened my eyes wide.

He'd been sitting quietly, listening all this time, and now he answered slowly, unconsciously, without even thinking about it.

"Not quite," he said dully. "Borden thought we wanted to play a practical joke on Weather. He got panicky after Jay's death and after you talked to him. He phoned me and went to pieces, and I—" he looked at his big hands— "had to take care of him." Hannibal shook his head. "God, I didn't start out to kill Weather, much less Borden. I wouldn't have if Gladys hadn't badgered me, and if it hadn't looked so perfect, and if the old fool hadn't gone to see . . . you . . ."

His voice faltered as, all of a sudden, it hit him. I wasn't supposed to ask questions—I *couldn't!* Fear stained his face and he jerked his head up to stare at me. He couldn't have been more surprised and shocked if I were a corpse that had suddenly risen from its casket.

His mouth dropped open and he gasped aloud.

I grinned at him.

"Yes, Hannibal," I said softly. "There are cops in the rooms on both sides of us taking all this down, and cops outside in the hall, and you're through."

He couldn't grasp it. It was too sudden, too unnerving. He'd been living with the memory of murder and hadn't liked that digging into him. And now this—all his carefully laid plans crumbling.

His face was blank for a long moment, his fists clenched; then he felt the solidity of the hypodermic in his hand and glanced at it. Footsteps pounded in the hall outside. Hannibal's face twisted and he got his legs under him and lunged toward me, bent far over with the point of that needle driving at me, and I grabbed the arms of the chair I sat in, jerked my legs up and planted both hard leather heels in the middle of his pretty face.

I slammed my feet solidly into him and the shock coursed up my legs and into my spine, but it stopped him and sent him staggering backward. The great, handsome length of him slipped to the floor, his face twisted and streaming blood, and as he crumpled to the carpet he still gripped the gleaming hypodermic he'd been ready to inject me with.

I never knew for sure whether he did it on purpose, or if he was just stunned, or if it was an accident in the way he fell, but he slammed the needle into the flesh at the side of his stomach and shoved the plunger home.

The door burst open, its lock splintered by heavy shoulders. Two plainclothes officers stumbled into the room, guns in their hands. Another officer was right behind them.

They took in everything with one quick glance and I yelled, "Get the bastard! He jabbed himself with that hypo."

From there on in, it was a walk.

18

Hannibal lasted fifteen or twenty minutes before he died, and even the dying part had been well thought out, only the guy who died in such a strange fashion was supposed to have been me. I hated to think how this might have turned out, considering what was in that vicious hypodermic, if I'd really gone into a hypnotic trance when I'd walked into the room.

A doctor had come in right on the heels of the police, but it didn't do any good. Hannibal talked like mad for a while, getting it off his chest, then anxiety grew in his face, and fear. Right at the end he was sorry he was going out—sorry for a lot of things—but even when the doctor knew what was wrong with him it was too late. Hannibal's pupils dilated and his hands started trembling. Then his arm muscles began twitching and perspiration flooded his face.

They tried, but they didn't even get him out of the hotel. He went into convulsions and collapsed, and it wasn't pretty to watch. Then he died.

That had been three hours ago. Now I was sitting in my car smoking a cigarette and thinking. I knew that the impetus behind the whole mess had been furnished by my recent love, Gladys, who was now cooling her heels in a cell. All the neat variations on the old murder theme had been supplied by the late Robert Hannibal, who had liked the way Gladys looked and the way she loved. I thought about the way Gladys looked and loved, and for a moment I was sorry for her. Then I remembered the rest of it and stopped feeling sorry at all.

I knew now that Hannibal had sent Lucian and Potter out of town, but they'd undoubtedly be picked up soon. I also knew I had been lucky that the inexpert Hannibal hadn't killed me Thursday night with an overdose from the first hypodermic he'd used on me then—but I was even luckier that he'd never got to use the second one—because it was full of adrenaline.

He'd had it all planned, even the suggestion he was going to give me. First a big slug of adrenaline in my veins; then I was supposed to leave the hotel and start running until my heart stopped and I dropped dead. L.A. DETECTIVE DROPS DEAD OF HEART FAILURE ON DOWNTOWN STREET. Hannibal was a cute bastard, all right.

I sat in the car and thought a lot more, but mostly I thought about Ann. She'd inherit everything now, but it wasn't going to be much consolation for her, not for a while. There was an awful lot of room in the big house on St. Andrews Place, particularly for such a little girl. It would take some time till she had completely recovered from this, and she was confused enough already. I hoped this didn't get her down too much. I liked Ann. I didn't know whether it was a good idea or not, but I started the car and headed for St. Andrews Place. She could always tell me to take off.

She answered the door. "Hi, Ann," I said. "I was out this way, so I stopped. See how you were, you know."

She smiled. "Come on in, Mark."

We sat on the divan in the living room. I noticed that most of the lights were burning downstairs, as if she were trying to erase all the shadows.

She said, "I'm glad you came by, Mark. I didn't like Gladys, but I still can't believe—" She broke it off and shook her head.

"Yeah. Pretty bad, I know. You all right?"

She smiled. "I'm all right. I feel sort of numb, that's all."

We talked a few more minutes, quietly and almost casually, and she asked a few questions about what had happened, just to get it straight in her mind, she said. I told her the things she wanted to know as briefly as possible.

Then she said, "You don't have to sit around with me, Mark. I'm all right, honest. I think maybe I'd like to be alone, get the crying over with. If I'm going to cry, that is. I really don't know."

She stopped for a moment, then glanced at me with an odd look on her face. "I've done a lot of thinking, Mark. About everything—about me, too.

Everything's mixed up, but I guess I hated Gladys too much, maybe. And loved Dad too much. Too much of everything." She stopped talking again and shrugged. "Skip it. That's not what I wanted to say, anyway. But thanks for coming tonight, Mark."

I got up to go. "Anything I can do, Ann . . ."

"I know."

"Maybe I'm stupid to mention it now," I said, "but if you feel up to it one of these days, maybe I can buy you another drink at Frankie's."

She smiled and her eyes crinkled a little. "I'd like that, Mark. I really would. And thanks."

I left her at the door, and she waved to me as I drove back toward town.

In the office, where it had all started, I sat behind my desk and wondered if I'd ever be quite the same again. It had been like a nightmare. I knew I hadn't committed murder, but the thought that it *could* have happened haunted me.

I couldn't help wondering how it would have ended if it hadn't been Hannibal, who wasn't expert in hypnotic technique, but Joseph Borden or somebody like Bruce Wilson, somebody who really knew how to control another person's mind. Or even what might have happened if Hannibal had been able to spend more time working on me. Enough more time so that I couldn't have recognized that posthypnotic suggestion to go to the Phoenix.

Even now that Hannibal and Gladys had talked, and I could account for almost all the things I'd done during the past three days, there were still little blank spots, still small gaps in my memory. Of course, I realized some of my knowledge was the knowledge I'd got from listening to the recording I'd made of that first session at the Phoenix Hotel. It wasn't as if I'd actually lived it, but like something that had happened to another person, something I'd just been told about. I wondered if this thing that had happened to me might have happened, with variations, to others; to others who might not have been as lucky in finding out as I had been; to others who never did learn that the impulses in their minds were really the suggestions of somebody else; or to others who simply didn't remember. I knew, now, that it could have happened to many persons who would laugh if such an apparently insane possibility were suggested to them.

I thought I had this whole picture put together now, but vague doubts were still with me. Just as sometimes you wonder where the dream ends and reality begins, I wondered which of my memories were real and which were false, what had actually happened and what hadn't.

Then I shook the momentary depression off. The hell with it, Logan. You've got the picture now. You can even check back, go over some of the ground again and check up on your actions and conversations. Should be easy, you're a detective.

I started feeling more like myself. Tomorrow I'd nose around a little, and in a few days I'd have everything pinned down tight. Get back to normal and then forget it, that was the thing. I was being an old maid, anyway. I knew damn well I'd talked to Gladys and Ann, Hannibal, Arthur, Peter and Ayla . . . yeah, Ayla.

That had been real enough. The only hypnosis there was in Ayla's white thighs. I couldn't have imagined the moist heat of her lips, the curve of her breasts, her long red fingernails. I couldn't have imagined that!

Of course, it wouldn't hurt to make sure. I could check up tomorrow just to make sure my memory wasn't playing tricks on me.

A mean-looking woman, Ayla. That foot swinging gently, obviously for effect. That smooth white thigh. Uh-huh. Have to check up on that tomorrow.

I grabbed the phone book, looked for the number and started dialing.

Hell, I was already back to normal. Why wait till tomorrow?

THE END

About the Author

RICHARD PRATHER is the author of the world famous Shell Scott detective series, which has over 40,000,000 copies in print in the U.S. and many millions more in hundreds of foreign–language editions. In 1986 he was awarded the Private Eye Writers of America's Life Achievement Award for his contributions to the Private Eyes Genre. He and his wife, Tina, live among the beautiful Red Rocks of Sedona, Arizona. He enjoys organic gardening, gin on the rocks, and golf. He collects books on several different life-enriching subjects and occasionally re-reads his own books with huge enjoyment, especially STRIP FOR MURDER.